INVOCATION

The Soul Scribe Trilogy, Book Two

Tera Lyn Cortez

TLC

ISBN: 978-1-7330171-2-1

www.teralyncortez.com

Original cover art by Violeta Nedkova

DEDICATION

For my children.
My life wouldn't be the same without you,
and I am so thankful for each of you.
Robbie, Jordan, Desirae, Hannah & Avery, I love you!

ACKNOWLEDGMENTS

When I first embarked on this journey I had little idea of what was actually in store for me. I still don't to be honest. But my sincere thanks go out to everyone who has been there for me along the way.

To those who have read my book, shared and reviewed my work, I wouldn't be able to do any of this without you. Thank you.

Chapter One

Consciousness snapped rudely into crystal-clear focus before I had even had a chance to open my eyes, and as soon as awareness found its way to my thoughts, I became overcome with anguish. In spite of my eyelids closed, the tears leaked through them. They made tracks down my cheeks, leaving tacky trails on my skin and pooling near my ears.

Every muscle in my body felt as if tied into knots. My very bones ached, and each joint seemed swollen beyond its capacity for function. The bodily pains could almost be considered tolerable, but I would have taken any level of physical torment in place of the gut-wrenching emotions that plagued me.

The air in the study still held a charge as if the magical storm wasn't completely past us yet. The stone floor pressed cold and hard against my back, and the uneven texture pushed against me through my clothes. I could hear Xavier and Taryk, although their voices were somewhat muffled as if they came from far away. The bright glow from above gave a telltale sign that Celeste hovered over me, and all I wanted was for each of them to disappear, so I could pretend this was all a nightmare of epic proportions.

"Everleigh, I'm so sorry," she said, "but you must get up. Amara sacrificed greatly to come to you in her last moments, *do not* allow her gift to be in vain. Open your eyes and look at me."

Groaning in response, I turned my head to the side, hoping she would give up and go away. Small, cool hands grasped my own, and pulled me upright. Curiosity got the better of me, and I opened my eyes just to see whose hands I held.

For the first time, she stood before me, solid, as if she had returned to actual flesh and blood. At this point, I could do nothing more than stare. She had the same look about her as she always had as a spirit, but her hands appeared no less tangible than my own clasped within them.

"How…" I breathed. "I don't understand."

"Once we have taken care of this, I will explain. But you *must* get up."

Pushing the pain aside, I stood with her help, Xavier and Taryk reaching out to steady me. Looking at them both, I saw pain that echoed my own, the tear tracks running down each of their cheeks were probably the mirror image of the ones on my face. I also saw determination. Unable to help myself, I had to look around once more, hoping to see my mother's figure in the room. There was no sign of her.

"Everleigh, your mother has just transferred her power to you. While you cannot perform the invocation until you are in the scribe's ancestral home in Myntas, you must accept the power into yourself. Because you hold two distinct types of magic, you must allow this new magic to become a part of you. Visualize your tapestry, and there will be new, loose, threads throughout. You must weave them in, essentially creating a bond between the magic and yourself. As strong as you can possibly make it."

Closing my eyes, I almost lost my concentration, seeing the purple of her threads intertwining with my own. But I did as Celeste said. Searching out each one, I took my time in weaving them into my tapestry as tightly as I could. So many fluttered there, it exhausted me to pull them in, but I was determined to see it through.

By the time I made certain I had finished, my body had about given out. Closing my eyes again, all I wanted was to find relief from the pain, both in my body and my heart. I opened my eyes to see Xavier and Taryk both watching me intently, and Celeste asking me if I felt all right. My last thought, before I crumpled to the ground was that I would never be all right again.

The next time I opened my eyes, I saw only the ceiling above my own bed. The physical pain had gone away entirely, but I could hardly bear the crushing weight of the pain in my soul. How had this happened? I just got her back. How could I ever live without her? Her return to my life had been so brief, nothing more than a tease of the relationship we should've had. The thought of leaving my bed made me nauseous, and I closed my eyes again.

I heard no other sounds in the cabin, and had no idea where the guys were or what they might've been doing. I didn't bother trying to use our bonds to find out. Rolling onto my side, facing away from the window and the waterfall, I curled into the tightest ball I could manage and wept.

The feelings of helplessness and loss surrounded me, dragging me back in time to the day I got the call that my adoptive parents had been in an accident. The person on the other end of the line let me know that an officer was on the way to my house and would arrive shortly. I remembered staring at my cell phone in disbelief, still thinking they were taking me to the hospital to see them.

I waited on the front porch swing that day, not knowing how drastically my life was about to change. I watched the patrol car as it made its way up our drive. Two officers exited the car, and I can remember being surprised that they felt two were necessary. I grabbed my purse, heading down the steps to meet them.

"Please hurry. I need to see them!"

The officers looked at each other, and one of them gently took my arm, guiding me back to the swing. "Ma'am, I'm so sorry, but neither of them survived the crash. The driver of the other vehicle never even hit the brakes. They died on impact, and if it makes you feel any better, they did not suffer."

I remember wondering at that moment how anything they could say would make me feel any better. The world around me began to spin, and everything went black at that point also. Apparently, I'm not very skilled at dealing with emotional trauma.

My bladder insisted I get out of bed, and yet I found it hard to believe there was any liquid left to empty, seeing as how it was all coming out my eyes. They felt grainy and full of sand. Tears made my vision blurry, but I had a choice to make. I was either getting up and crossing the hall to the bathroom or wetting my bed for the first time since I turned three.

I elected to get out of bed just to use the toilet, simply to avoid having to lay in a wet smelly bed for the next few days. I had no intention of getting up when I barely wanted to continue living.

Struggling to gather the willpower to sit up, I managed to swing my legs over the side of the bed. The physical strength of my body shocked me. Had it not been for the pain in my heart, I would have felt like a million bucks. Crossing the hall, I took a quick glance into the main room, but saw no sign of either Taryk or Xavier. After performing the necessary bodily functions, I stood in front of the mirror and stared at myself. My eyes, so much like my mother's, stared back at me. I leaned forward, hands resting on either side of the mirror.

"Mom… How did this happen? What am I supposed to do without you? I can't do this alone."

"Everleigh…"

My head snapped around, positive I had just heard her voice. Of course, she was not there, but I wanted to believe she was so badly. And then I heard her again.

"Everleigh, you are not alone. You will never be alone. Remember that. Xavier and Taryk will be by your side, and I will *always* be with you. You were born for this. You have everything you need to be successful. You just have to believe in yourself. I love you."

Her voice faded away before I was ready to let her go. I called for her again and again, but she did not answer. The next thing I knew there was knocking at the bathroom door.

"Ev… are you okay in there?"

I cried so hard, I couldn't get the words out to answer him. The door opened a crack, and Taryk peered in. He managed to catch me just as I sagged to the floor, sitting with me and pulling me gently into his lap. He seemed to know that I needed—no words, just wrapped his arms around me and held me while I mourned.

His chin rested on the top of my head, and at some point, I became aware of his heartbeat beneath my ear. As my sobs quieted, I noticed that my heart matched the rhythm of his perfectly. My breaths calmed to be even and deep, again, matching his.

After a while, I was sure he had to be sore with the hard floor digging into him and my added weight on top of that. Yet, he never once complained or attempted to move. He just sat there, arms wrapped around me as I tried to gather the strength needed to not only move on with my daily life, but somehow be the person the realms needed me to be.

Pulling back slightly, I looked up at his face, reaching out to cup his cheek with my hand and meeting his deep blue eyes. I had no words for him, but I knew in my heart we didn't need any. Had I any doubts before about my magic's choice in a mate, they were no longer. And while I had zero interest in a romantic relationship right now, it gave me strength to know that I had a partner to help get through the dark days ahead.

Xavier would stand beside us, and we would prevail. I could not let my mother down, not when she had sacrificed so much for me. Her entire life had been lived to ensure mine could be all that it was meant to be. Her sacrifices gave me the push I needed to move forward, and I would do my best to make her proud. Wherever she existed now, I hoped she was at peace.

Just as we made the effort to rise off the floor, my stomach let out a noisy growl, causing Taryk to smile.

"Well, apparently your appetite hasn't changed."

I had to give a little grin in return. The truth of the matter was that I needed to keep on living, and in order to do so, I needed food. He took my hand, giving it a quick squeeze, and led me to the living room, settling me on the couch.

"I've got breakfast handled. You sit and rest."

"Where is Xavier?" I hadn't seen nor heard any sign of him since opening my eyes.

"He went out." Taryk's forehead wrinkled as he told me. "I think he just needed some time to process things. I'm sure he'll be back."

I reached out to him along our bond, searching. I felt him out there, sadness washing over me in waves that made me catch my breath. His pain very nearly mirrored my own. He sat next to the waterfall, and I wanted to go to him, but couldn't decide if it was safe for me to do so.

Although at this point, someone, somewhere, must've known that my mother had given her powers over. I hardly figured the fact that she had an heiress remained a secret. We probably didn't have long before evil would be knocking at our door.

Deciding it was best to give him time, I sent love and comfort through our bond as best I could and left him to his grief. Taryk brought me a plate heaping with my favorite breakfast foods, and I did my best to open our bond and let my feelings pour through, so he knew just how grateful I felt. The bonds were allowing me to connect with those I loved when words failed me.

Xavier came through the front door just as I put my plate in the kitchen sink. He came straight to me, wrapped me in a hug, and we just stood there together. I leaned into him with my head against his chest, feeling the rhythm of his heart beating, and knowing we were hurting in a way that only time would lessen.

These two would be my strength as I would try to be for them. I needed all the help I could get to come out the victor in the battle looming ahead, and there was no time like the present to begin preparing.

Chapter Two

I let them know that I needed to go to the study to talk to Celeste since she had promised to give me some answers, before I so rudely passed out on her. I wanted to see what she had to say about the situation, and I *really* wanted to know how she had managed to manifest herself physically right after my mother had appeared.

First though, I decided to have a shower. Not only would it make me feel a little better, I admit I hoped to hear my mother's voice again. I'm not sure why the bathroom would have been her choice of places, but I wasn't going to argue. I'd take whatever I could get at this point.

Stopping in my room to grab clean clothes, since I had been in these same ones for far too long, I headed into the bathroom and turned on the shower. Once I had it running, and I could be relatively sure the guys wouldn't hear me from the front room, I said her name very softly.

"Mom? I don't know what I am going to do without you. Are you in here? Can you hear me?" I stood in front of the mirror in the growing cloud of steam for what seemed like hours, but I received no response. As sad as it made me that it had been a one-time thing, I realized how blessed I felt to have heard her voice that last time. And maybe, if I got really lucky, it wouldn't be the last time after all.

I had planned to take a long, hot shower, but realized I couldn't spend too much time in there with nothing to occupy my brain, or I would sink to the floor and weep. Get out. Dry off. Get dressed.

I had to remind myself repeatedly to put one foot in front of the other so I could keep moving forward. I didn't have the luxury of dawdling. I needed to keep a tight rein on my emotions, or they would get the better of me in a heartbeat, and I couldn't allow that. If I lost control now, who knew how long it would take me to get it back.

Leaving the bathroom, I headed down the hall to the study, hoping to have a conversation with Celeste. The door swung open silently, as it always had, and I first looked for her presence. Since I didn't see her, I called her name softly.

"Celeste? Are you in here?"

Nothing but silence greeted me, and I began to wonder if something had happened and she could no longer remain in the study. I couldn't accept losing someone else in such a short time and called her name again. I was stymied by the silence, as she had never neglected to answer me in at least some way.

I glanced around the study, taking it in as if I had never seen it before. Staring at the spot where I had last seen my mother's image almost drove me to my knees. At least I had not watched my adoptive parents go. The phone call and police visit I received was horrific, but nothing like watching the life fade from the eyes of someone you loved.

I ran my fingers along the edge of the scribe book as I passed, taking comfort from the fact that I could open it and see my mother's handwriting there. I wondered if the date of her death would automatically populate, or if I would be responsible for writing it in the appropriate spot.

There had been no mention of a cemetery for scribes, and I wondered where their final resting place ended up being. In this case, at least, there would be no funeral. Although I felt like a celebration of her life would be in order once all was calm in the realms again.

As I walked down the stone tunnel to the training room, I passed the vault that held all the items from my father. So much of it still needed to be gone through, and I knew important things waited to be discovered.

As I passed the second closed door, I wondered what it held. Jiggling the door handle, I found it locked, and made a mental note to ask Xavier if he knew what the room held.

I trailed my hand along the rough stone wall as I walked the remainder of the tunnel. I attempted to connect with the Earth and the mountain itself. I drew in a sharp breath to see Celeste seated in the middle of the cavernous room, looking as if she was meditating.

She had returned to her more ethereal appearance, but nothing indicated that she struggled to maintain herself visually. Her eyes didn't open immediately, but she smiled as I approached her.

"Please, sit down, Everleigh." She opened her eyes and waved me to the spot directly in front of her.

"I can see you." Articulate I may not have been, but I excelled at stating the obvious.

"Many things changed when your mother appeared before us. I know you have many questions, and I will answer what I can."

"You were here. Really here. I could feel your hands as if they were as solid as my own. How?"

"In order to project her appearance here, your mother wielded an immense amount of power. Her spirit crossed the realms, and in doing so, she brought much of that intensity into the study. As I explained to you before, manifesting myself visually requires great expenditure of power. I simply did not have the amount required to become physically present. When your mother returned to her body, much of the magic she used remained in the study, trapped, for lack of a better term. I harnessed it and employed it to give myself a physical presence because I believed you needed it."

For a moment, I just stared. I vaguely recalled feeling the magic stirring the air around me as I came to. I hadn't realized at the time that it was residual.

"I did need it, thank you. The shock of seeing you actually in front of me is what propelled me to return to the present. Had I been given a choice at that moment, I think I would have chosen to shrivel up and disappear."

I wrapped my arms around my legs and sank my forehead to my knees. I took a deep breath and tried to get control of the emotions raging inside me. Emotions were proving to be more difficult to control than magic.

“I know you are hurting. Emotional pain is one of the few things that magic has no jurisdiction over. But don't let it consume you. Use it as a driving force. Put it to work for good. We need to prepare for your invocation.”

I looked up. “I thought I had to be twenty-one.”

Celeste shook her head sadly. “When power is passed on because of a death, the heiress immediately becomes eligible for the invocation. The realms must have a reigning scribe.”

“We had no time to talk about it, so I don't know what needs to be done.” It was a stark reminder of the many things we would never discuss.

“The ceremony must be performed at the scribe chateau in Myntas. There is a specific room where every invocation has taken place. Its sole purpose is the invocation of the next scribe. Normally the reigning scribe performs the ritual, but you are able to perform it for yourself.”

I needed to master the art of creating portals in a hurry. If I had to start gallivanting through the other realms to visit all these places, I'd better learn how to get there in once piece. The less confrontations we ran into, the better! So far, the two places we needed to go were highly protected. I just needed to get there without drawing too much attention to myself before I was ready.

"Are there instructions for how the ceremony is performed, and what I need to do before I am able to conduct it?"

"Yes, there are instructions. I can go over it with you. There are also step-by-step directions located in the ceremony room. Everything you need for the induction itself can be found there as well."

"I would feel so much better if you could be with me. I feel like I need so much help, and I am terrified that I'm going to fail the realms. What if I make an irreversible mistake?"

I seemed to fluctuate rapidly between being confident I could live up to everything people expected of me and being absolutely certain of abject failure before I ever began. It made me feel manic depressive with the terrifying highs and lows that seemed to interchange by the moment.

Celeste gave me a small smile. "I am working on a way that you may, indeed, be able to take me with you."

I searched her face with obvious curiosity and nurtured the tiny flame of hope that sparked inside me. "Really?"

She stood, indicating I should do the same and I followed her to the study. "I believe there is a way. I originally bound my soul to this place, successfully, which is why I can be here for you now. I am going to attempt to attach my soul instead to an object, perhaps a piece of jewelry, so I can travel with you outside of the mountain. The power I absorbed gave me the ability to manifest myself visually as I wish with no repercussions. I do not become tired or fade away unless I wish it."

I grinned and found myself wishing I could hug her. "Let me know what you need me to do, and I will do it. I can't tell you how much this means to me."

She nodded gracefully. "Perhaps choose a piece of jewelry that you enjoy and wouldn't mind wearing constantly while we are traveling. Make it something sturdy, so we don't worry about it getting broken and falling off, yet fairly inconspicuous so that it is not an object that garners too much unwanted attention."

"There are chests full of jewelry in the vault that holds my inheritance from my father. We need to go through it anyway, and I am sure we can find a suitable piece among the jewels there. I'll get the guys and begin searching."

"While you do that, I am attempting to find a way to aid you in learning to create portals. It would be the safest way for you to travel."

Thanking her, I headed to the front of the cabin to meet with the guys and lay out a path for success. Bolstered by the possibility of having Celeste along on our journeys, and strengthened by the anger at whomever had taken my mother from me, I seethed with impatience to make myself known. Someone was going to pay for what they had done.

I seated myself in the kitchen chair between them and rested my elbows on the table. Taryk immediately slid the plate of crackers and cheese he had been snacking on my direction. He certainly learned quickly.

"Okay, gentlemen. Let's get a game plan in order. We need to finish going through the vault for two reasons. A, my intuition tells me there are still things in there that we need to take with us. And B, I need an appropriate piece of jewelry for Celeste to connect herself to. She believes that because she successfully bound her soul to this location, she should also be able to bind herself to an object. In this way, she can travel with us throughout the realms."

Both of them raised their brows, seemingly surprised at my revelation. Taryk nodded thoughtfully, and Xavier appeared to be mulling over the possibilities.

"I think we can find something. Perhaps a bracelet? That seems to be the safest choice, since we can spell it to ensure it doesn't leave your wrist, and we don't have to be concerned about losing her along the way." I could tell Xavier was already running through the options in his mind.

I grinned. "Great minds think alike, big brother."

The three of us stood in unison, heading toward the vault. Taryk's hand rested lightly on my back as he allowed me to pass him and lead the way, leaving me feeling a little warm and fuzzy inside. I could feel the heat of his palm through my T-shirt, and it led to a warmth in my stomach that I was unaccustomed to. I liked it.

Drawing near the vault door, I paused.. "Hey,Xavier, do you know what is hidden behind door number two?" I pointed toward it in a game show hostess impression.

"No," he rolled his eyes at me, "I haven't got a clue. I don't know if your mother has ever opened it."

Of course, that ignited my imagination, and I stood before it instead of heading directly into the vault. I placed both hands on the heavy wood, hoping my intuition would chime in and give me a clue. Strangely enough, I got nothing. It almost seemed as if the door itself had been shielded to avoid giving off any indications at all.

Frowning, I leaned my forehead against it and closed my eyes, pushing deeper. I could feel something just out of reach, like a slippery little fish I couldn't quite get a hold of.

“We need to see what is in there. It would only have the protections it does if it held something important.”

Heading into the vault, we agreed on a division of labor. The guys would go through the chests of jewelry looking for a suitable piece while I wandered about waiting for something to give off an impression of importance.

I walked slowly, opening my mind to the objects hidden within the chests and sacks scattered throughout the room. I physically touched as many of them as I could reach, running my fingertips over materials that had last been touched centuries ago.

Taryk held up a gorgeous jeweled bangle for my inspection, asking if it could be suitable for Celeste to use.

I shook my head. “Too ostentatious. I want to love it, since it won't be coming off, but I don't want everyone else to want it also. It can't draw too much attention.”

Coming to a stop before a tall armoire, one that rose above my head by a good six inches, my curiosity engaged. Pulling it open, I gasped in awe. It held gorgeous gowns. Reaching out, I couldn't help but run my fingers through them, marveling at the texture of the silks. Pulling one from the group, I held it up to myself. It appeared to be exactly my size.

Xavier looked over at me and laughed. “Playing dress up when you should be working, huh?” He stood and wandered over to me. “Father was a huge fan of buying my mother gowns. He loved to see her dressed in the finest he could find, and had materials brought in from every realm.”

Hanging it back with its comrades, I sighed. “Perhaps there will be a time when it will be appropriate to wear such finery. But this is definitely not that day.”

He reached toward the back and pulled out a particularly splendid one. “This is a traditional Fae wedding gown.” He waggled his eyebrows at me and inclined his head toward Taryk.

“Well, I certainly won't be needing that any time soon.”

Taryk ignored the implication and held up another option for Celeste's bracelet. This time it was perfect. The cuff was not too wide, made of polished silver and inset with tiny clear stones. I slipped it on and instantly fell in love.

“What do you think Xavier?”

He nodded. “Once her soul is bound to it, we can alter the size to be sure it will fit snugly to your wrist, and I think it will fit the bill perfectly.”

They guys headed toward the door, yet an odd feeling held me back. Something was calling to me, almost demanding my attention, although I couldn't get a sense of where it was coming from.

“Hey, Xavier? Is there anything in this room that you can feel, maybe that's not normal?”

He turned to me, brows raised. “Not normal?”

Taryk stopped next to him, both of them watching me with inquisitive looks. The words to describe what I felt were lost to me, but I made an attempt..

“I feel as if there is an object here that is endeavoring to get my attention, for lack of a better way to say it. The thought just kind of hovers in the back of my mind, unless I think about leaving the room, or being elsewhere. Then it gets more insistent. A s if it's trying to tell me not to leave without it. But I can't pinpoint where exactly it's coming from.”

As they stood near the door, I could tell they each worked to identify the feeling I was attempting to explain. They wore almost identical looks of concentration, eye scanning the room. In the end, they both shook their heads.

“Sorry, Ev,” Taryk said. “Not an inkling of anything for me.” Xavier shrugged and nodded his agreement.

“You guys go on ahead, maybe give the bracelet to Celeste. I'll follow you in a few. I just want to see if I can find what seems to be so important in here.”

As they left the room, I sat cross-legged in the middle of the crates and chests. Closing my eyes, I did my best to call forth the tiny voice in my head that didn't want to be left behind.

For a few moments, I couldn't seem to hone in on any area in particular. Pulling up my sight, I noticed a very small chest in one of the back corners seemed to have its own aura. Varying shades of green appeared to be leaking out of the box itself. Curious, I positioned myself on the floor in front of it and laid my hand on it.

The lid opened a crack at the contact, inviting me to open it the rest of the way and see what lay inside. There, on a miniature bed of silk, lay the most perfect tiny doll I had ever seen. She was no taller than my hand was long. I reached down and laid a finger on the tiny shoe, marveling at its preciseness. At the contact, she began to glow brightly. A few seconds later, she sat up and came to life!

“Oh my God!” Jerking my hand out of the crate, I accidentally knocked the lid closed.

Chapter Three

After a few seconds of silence, I heard her speak. “Um, hello? It's dark in here.” Her tiny muffled voice floated out from the confines of the box.

Reaching out, I opened the lid again, staring inside in disbelief. “I'm sorry, I really am so sorry, but... Who are you? And what are you doing in there? How *long* have you been in there?”

Craning her neck to look up at me, she smiled. “You must be King Oseron's daughter. He told me only you would be able to rouse me from my long sleep.”

I stared at her perfect little self, speechless and astounded. Had she really been in this crate since my father was alive? That struck me as being so cruel.

"I've surprised you, I'm sorry. It's obvious you had no idea I waited for you here. Your father sent me to be your guide. When you return to the original castle in Amarys, I am to be your escort. I am a wood sprite of the royal clan; our family has ruled the woods surrounding the castle for as long as it has been in existence. We continued to do so even after the king and his queen constructed their new residence closer to town. I am Princess Yurielle."

"My name is Everleigh. Have you really been lying in there for all these years?"

"When King Oseron chose me as the volunteer to fill this roll, he explained the situation. My body and soul would be put into stasis and sent here to await your need of me. I was told that your proximity to my resting place would be enough to trigger the spell that would draw your attention."

"It certainly did that. Now that you are awake, what can I do for you? You must need food or drink, and maybe some time to stretch your wings and get moving?"

"That is very kind of you, however it is I who is here to serve you, Princess. What may I help you with?"

"Oh no. Stop right there. While I am thankful you're here, since I can use all the help I can get, let's get one thing straight. You are *not* here to *serve* me. And I am not a princess. Just Everleigh will be fine."

She looked slightly taken aback at my statement, and then confused. Her reluctance to question me was evident by the look on her face, however her need to understand the situation won out.

“You are King Oseron's daughter, are you not?” I nodded, and she continued. “And … all daughters of kings are customarily princesses, are they not?”

I stared at her, pretty sure my chin was resting on the stone floor in surprise. Holy crap. I knew Xavier was a prince. And that his father, the king, was also my father. But never in the name of all that was holy had I considered the ramifications of those relationships.

“Well, since you put it that way, I suppose you are correct. I hadn't thought about it like that.”

She laughed, a merry little tinkling sound that brought my spirits up just hearing it. “Would you like to see your tiara?”

I watched her, mouth agape, as she flew up to the wardrobe that held the fancy dresses. “Right in this drawer.”

Pulling open the drawer she indicated revealed a silver box. I lifted the hinged lid and gasped in astonishment. It was gorgeous.

“This... this is mine?”

“Your father had it made specifically for you when he knew he would be having a daughter. I believe there are many spells laid upon it for your safety and happiness as well, but I cannot attest to which ones.”

I ogled it for a few seconds more, then closed the box and the drawer. Now that I knew what had been so important in the vault, we needed to get moving. And I had to introduce my new friend to the others.

“Would you like to meet King Oseron's son?”

Her little face lit up like a Christmas tree. “He has other children still living? When he told me of the future that had been foreseen by the visionary, he was certain that none of the family would survive, other than you.”

“Only one. Xavier was captured, and held prisoner fora long time by the mage who murdered his family. When he escaped, my mother found him and brought him here so he would be safe.”

Her wings drooped, and her face lost the look of excitement it had previously held. “So sad...”

“He's amazing, though. You'll love him. Come meet him.”

Closing the door to the vault as we left, I explained to her about where she had found herself after sleeping for all those years. As we got closer, I held up my finger to indicate we should be quiet.

“I want them to be surprised when they see you.”

I got another one of her infectious giggles as she replied, “I have no doubt they will be.”

When we reached the study, Xavier, Taryk, and Celeste were huddled around the workbench with their backs to us. I assumed they were working on the bracelet. Motioning Yurielle behind me, I approached the group.

“Hey, guys. There's someone I'd like you to meet.”

Three inquiring faces turned to greet me, perplexed when they saw I stood alone.

"Uh, and where did you find this new friend, Ev?" Taryk eyed me suspiciously as I stood there with a grin on my face.

Moving aside, I introduced her. "Guys, this is Yurielle. Yurielle, meet Celeste, Taryk, and my brother Xavier."

She said hello to the group, curtsying cutely to Xavier as she hovered in the air. "Please, call me Yuri. It's an honor to meet you, Your Highness."

Xavier backed up till he bumped into the table, shaking his head the whole time. "Oh, no, no, no." He gestured somewhat wildly with both hands as he spoke. "Please, just call me Xavier. Please."

Yuri looked between the two of us, confused. "So, I have a princess who didn't even know she is a princess, and a prince who doesn't want to be a prince? I'm not sure I understand the situation."

I had to laugh. She got a quick rundown of what had been going on while she slumbered as we returned to the workbench so they could finish their work on the bracelet.

After Xavier had performed a ritual to cleanse the bracelet of any other magic or energy, Celeste prepared to cast the same spell she had used to tether her soul to the study upon the bangle. Before she began, she looked at me and seemed as if she wanted to speak but hesitated.

"What do you need, Celeste?" I wanted her to feel as if she could ask me anything, but I did not want her to feel as if I was pushing her either.

"If you are willing, I would like to attempt to forge a bond between us, as you have done with Xavier and Taryk. I believe that such a connection could be invaluable as we travel throughout the other realms."

"I don't know why I never thought of that. Of course, I am willing. Let's do it right now. Do you think there is anything I need to be wary of before I begin?"

She shook her head. "I don't believe so. Bonds are created between souls, and I think the process should be exactly the same."

"Okay. I usually attempt to make physical contact since that seems to give my magic extra oomph. This time, though, I will sit and call up my sight to create the bond. As I am doing so, I'd like you to make contact with me in any way you feel comfortable. I think that will be enough."

I settled on the stone floor where I had been standing. Crossing my legs and closing my eyes, I focused my vision, searching for Celeste's thread. Hers were created of a myriad of color, much the same as mine, but in softer, more muted tones. Whereas my own were bold jewel tones, hers were more pastel, and in fewer shades. It was breathtaking.

Whether because we were related, or because our tapestries were so similar, I had no problem creating a strong bond. The strands wove effortlessly together, and it took only a few brief moments before I opened my eyes and grinned at her.

“Don't get up yet.” Yuri landed on my knee. “Your Highness, I request the gift of bonding with you as well. If it does not offend.”

She looked toward the floor, almost as if she were embarrassed to have asked. I reached out gently, lifting her chin so she looked at me once more.

“On one condition. No, make that two conditions.” I looked her at her sternly, almost feeling bad for teasing her as her expression became guarded. “One, you may never again treat me as if I am above you. We are equals, and I am grateful to have you here.”

Her eyes widened in surprise.

“And two, STOP CALLING ME YOUR HIGHNESS!” I laughed out loud as she put her hands on her tiny hips and glared at me.

“Try to boss me around, will you?!” The glint in her eye was the only warning I had before she lifted a tiny hand to her mouth and puffed a short burst of air in my direction.

Tiny sparkles rained down on my face, first causing me to sneeze repeatedly, and then igniting uncontrollable laughter. Her wings fluttered as she hovered above me while I giggled until my ribs ached. I could hear everyone else laughing in the background, and at first, I assumed she had gotten them as well. Then I realized they were all laughing *at me*!

“I'm … sorry … please … make it … stop!” I could hardly form an entire word, much less a coherent sentence.

As the giggles wound down, I took a deep breath and attempted to regain some semblance of my dignity.

Xavier leaned against the worktable, smirking in my direction. “Ev hasn't had any dealings with a wood sprite before,” he explained, nodding in Yuri's direction. “She has no idea what she's in for.”

Deciding that now was as good a time as any to pretend to establish the pecking order, I called up a tiny shield and encased her in the bubble. Laughing, I teased her.

“Not such hot stuff now, are you?”

She just smirked at me, and Xavier, Taryk, and Celeste all backed further away. I had a moment of concern at their reaction but held my ground. She raised her tiny little hands, facing her palms in my direction, and I could see her mouthing words, although she did not say them out loud.

I laughed at the look of surprise on her face when nothing happened. She stuck her tongue out at me from inside her little prison, and I smiled, releasing her.

“Are we even?” I asked, reaching out to shake on it.

“Oh no,” she shook her little head emphatically. “We are not even. However, I shall wait until you do not expect retaliation before I pounce.” She tried to look menacing, but her eyes were smiling, and I knew in that moment I had found a valuable friend.

Chapter Four

Yuri and I cemented our bond, and it surprised me how earthy her threads were. Varying shades of brown and green were prevalent, and strands of blue occasionally appeared. I learned more about soul tapestries with each one I encountered.

All of us with physical bodies were starving and headed to the kitchen to eat while Celeste completed her spell to move the binding from the study to the bracelet. Then we planned to test it to ensure she really could go anywhere the bracelet went before binding it to my wrist.

The three of us took turns on catching Yuri up with more details of all that had been going on since she had been lying dormant in the vault. We also laid out a tentative plan of how to complete the most pressing tasks.

"Most importantly, I need to learn how to create portals, so we can safely visit two places. First, the scribe chateau in Myntas, so my invocation can be performed. Second, the ancestral castle in Amarys, to find the hidden room and the items Father left for me. Anything else that needs to be added to the priority list?"

"While we are in Amarys, if we can make contact with my family, they will no doubt have excellent intel on what the mage has been up to there." Yuri looked thoughtful as she paced the tabletop.

"I think we will have to take stock of the situation before we decide whether to leave the safety of the castle. The woods surrounding it have no protections, and we will be vulnerable to attack once we leave the castle walls." Xavier looked concerned at the very suggestion.

"I agree, that is something we will need to decide after we get the lay of the land, so to speak." Taryk also seemed unnerved by the prospect.

"Your high- ahem, Everleigh?" She made a face as if she choked on the very words leaving her mouth but managed to catch herself before completing the phrase.

I laughed a little at her displeasure but acknowledged her effort. "Yes?"

"You should have no trouble creating a portal since you wear the ring. Have you tried it yet? The ring was blessed by the greatest master of portals that ever lived."

I frowned at the reminder that I had, indeed, attempted to make one, but was unsuccessful. Which I let Yuri know.

"First, you must awaken the ring. Its powers have been lying dormant for many years. It is a simple spell, but one that must be performed by you alone, since you will be the one to wield its power. I will teach you the spell when we return to the study."

I felt a little better knowing there was an explanation aside from my own incompetence that had prevented me from creating the portal during my earlier experiment.

We finished the meal, brainstorming the items we would need to take with us on our journey to the other realms. Yuri was a consistent source of enjoyment, teasing and joking throughout the conversation.

Returning to the study, we found Celeste smiling her satisfaction. "It is done."

Picking up the bracelet from the worktable, I headed to the front of the cabin to see if she could now leave the study. She hovered alongside me for the entire walk down the hall, which she had not been able to do since she bound herself to the study.

"I have not seen these rooms in centuries. The structure itself has not changed." She floated toward the window. "How I have missed the view of the falls."

I stood silently and waited for her to have her moment. I couldn't fathom what it must have been like to wait centuries in the study, remaining unknown. She had zero social interaction for all that time and must have been so lonely. My heart swelled with gratitude for what she had endured in order to be here for me.

Again, I contemplated the number of people who had begun

preparing for my battle long before I had even been born. My mother spent her *entire life* preparing for mine. There were people who gave their magic over so I may inherit it. People who sacrificed their autonomy to be my guide, like Yuri. Celeste gave up her eternal rest to wait for me. My father spent the years before his death gathering items that would help me to be successful. And there was a good chance that there were others I didn't even know about yet. It was mind boggling.

Celeste turned to me, and we headed to the study so the planning could continue. I was in a hurry to get this show on the road.

Yuri pounced the moment we walked in the door. “Let’s awaken the ring, so you will be able to create the portals we need to travel. Taryk and Xavier have filled me in while you were absent, and I believe the time we have to prepare is running short.”

She had made it a quarter of the way down the stone hallway to the training room before she had even finished the sentence. I followed, grinning, as the boys hastened to catch up.

I removed the ring, holding it in the palm of my hand, as she instructed me on how to wake the powers held within.

“Close your eyes. Attempt to identify the essence of the ring. It is not alive, and does not have a soul, so it will not be the same as identifying a thread and weaving it with yours. Open your heart, and let it find you. It is meant for you, and the magic will call to you, but it will be so very softly at first. Even though it has no soul, it is almost sentient. It will only join you if it feels you are deserving of its power.”

Closing my eyes, I held it, waiting for some inkling of the action

I should take next. All I could hear was silence, aside from the shuffling of feet as the guys waited anxiously for a sign that whatever I was doing was working. I tried to tune them out, but they began whispering as they waited.

Opening my eyes, I glared at them pointedly. “I think the two of you should wait in the living room. Grab the bracelet so Celeste can go with you if she wants. I can't think with the racket you two are making.”

“Racket?” Xavier got only that one word out before Yuri was on him, chasing them off.

“She said OUT. Go.”

I noticed that when she got extremely worked up, she gave off a golden-green glow. Her tiny hands shooed them out almost as fast as her wings fluttered, and I couldn't help but smile. That little lady was a force to be reckoned with, and I was pleased to have her on my side.

I settled myself on the floor, and she, in turn, situated herself on my knee. “Try again. You can do it.”

Closing my eyes once more, I did my best to still my mind and allow my intuition to guide me. Unfortunately, my intuition seemed to be on vacation, because I was getting absolutely nothing.

Minutes dragged on as I tried to catch a hint of the “essence” I had been instructed to feel for. I looked at Yuri and frowned.

“Maybe it's broken? I am getting nothing. At all. No hint, or whisper, or even a whiff.”

She shook her head and put her hands on her hips. "Nope. Not broken. You just need to focus. Try again."

Wrinkling my forehead at her sassy demand, I did as I was told. Not that it made a difference. I still couldn't feel anything.

I flopped backward, stretching out on the training mat. I was frustrated and getting cranky. "You know what?"

She glanced at me, brows raised, but said nothing.

"Maybe I need to be *wearing* the ring. Maybe it needs to feel *my* essence."

I didn't wait for her response, I just tried it. Once the ring settled into place on my hand, I opened my mind, but instead of trying to draw the ring in, I pushed myself outward. I offered the aura of my spirit instead.

Almost immediately, I could feel the whispers of the power held within the stone. Yuri was silent, and I just kind of allowed myself to float there, not asking for anything, just waiting. I knew the exact moment the ring had accepted me by the power and knowledge that suddenly existed in my brain.

I scramble to get off the floor, almost mowing over Yuri in the process. "Oh! I'm sorry!" I slowed, chagrined, but she just laughed her merry little laugh.

"Something tells me you may have figured it out. I told you, you could do it." She smirked at me, and I made a sassy face back.

“Let’s make a portal into the living room and surprise the guys.” I held up my hand to begin, when she planted herself in front of it.

“Hold on there, missy. Portals require a huge energy output. They are not as easy as they seem. It will take some practice to perfect the skill.”

“Okay, I get it. I'm going to start practicing right now.” Ever so confidently, I lifted my hand and allowed the intuition I gleaned from the ring to take the lead.

The portal opened on the first try and I could see into the living room where the guys were sitting, and Celeste stood by the window. Throwing a smug look in her direction, I stepped toward it, but lost my concentration. The portal snapped shut, and I bounced off, landing on my butt with a thud.

Yuri fluttered directly above my face, eyebrows raised and expression smug. “I see you didn't bother to hold it open long enough to get through.”

“What happened to it?” I didn't understand where I had gone wrong. It opened so effortlessly.

“As I *tried* to tell you before. Naturally occurring portals just need to be accessed. You expend energy to open them, pass through, then expend more energy to close them. When you are creating your own portal, you must power it constantly. Once they are opened you must focus on holding them open long enough to get from one side to the other. They only exist as long as you are consciously willing them to do so.”

My head already ached from the effort of opening the portal the first time, but there was no way I was going to walk down the hallway to get to the living room. I could create a portal, and I was going to use it.

To keep my surprise from the guys, I elected to make a portal to the study as practice. Opening it was smooth sailing, just like the first time. And just like the first time the opening closed itself within seconds of appearing.

At the rate this particular skill was sapping my energy, we had better not ever need two in a row in a hurry. I already questioned my ability to even hold one long enough for all of us to make it through. I kept trying, and they kept closing on their own.

As usual, my stubbornness prodded me to try again. This time I held it open for a count of ten, which I figured would get us all through if we were quick. But the effort cost me, and I sank to the floor as my knees buckled underneath me.

Looking at Yuri, I sighed. "I don't know how I can do this more than once without using up most of my energy."

"Practice. You must build up endurance just as with every other skill. Because opening portals across longer distances requires even more energy."

Of course, it did. Struggling to my feet, I grimaced. Yuri positioned herself at head height in front of me and rubbed her hands together. Opening them she blew on her palms, and a silvery dust floated through the air, right into my face. I coughed, then sneezed just like the dust that had made me laugh. But this time, after taking a deep breath, I realized I no longer felt so tired.

“It is only temporary, but it will help.”

“Thank you.” I faced the wall giving me the shortest path to the living room and opened the portal. Yuri didn't hesitate to zip through, and I was right behind her, needing only a single step to pass through.

Both guys looked up in surprise, and Celeste smiled her serene smile. I had done it.

“Ev! You did it. I can't believe it.” Xavier threw his arms around me in a hug.

“Gee, thanks for the vote of confidence,” I chided him.

“You know what I mean.” He just kept grinning at me. “You know I'm proud of you, baby sister.”

“Hmm... Thanks to Yuri, I have energy left over. I say we each grab the things we will need to take with us and pack them up. We need to get ready and get on our way. Time isn't going to slow down while we piddle around here.”

Taryk shrugged as Yuri nodded in agreement. Xavier just smiled. “I think you are the only one who needs to gather anything other than weapons. Taryk and I will head to the training room and decide which ones we need to take. We will find supplies in the castle, and I am sure the chateau will have some as well. Celeste obviously doesn't need anything. Yuri, you good?”

“Yes, I will take Everleigh to the vault to grab a couple of other things, and then we will be ready."

Yuri and I entered the vault as the boys continued down the walkway to the training room. I had grabbed my backpack on the way in, so we would have someplace to store the stuff we picked up. Hopefully, it would be big enough.

First thing I grabbed was the leather holsters for my daggers since we had left them lying over a crate. I needed to change my clothes before I put them on.

I was wearing the ring, and Xavier would tighten the bracelet for me before we left. I couldn't imagine anything else I would need to take with me, but I also hadn't seen everything that occupied the room either.

Yuri pointed to the wardrobe chest holding the gowns. "Bring your tiara."

"What? No. I don't need a tiara. We are preparing for war. Where on Earth would I wear a tiara? What else do I actually *need?*"

She flew into my face, poking me in the nose with her tiny finger. "Bring. The. Tiara. Wrap it in a shirt and put it in your pack if you must. But bring it. I was sent here to help you, *Your Highness,* and if you don't listen to me, I won't be much assistance."

"Sheesh. Okay. Bossy much?" She just winked at me as I pulled it from its drawer.

She darted across the room, returning with one of the silk bags. "Take it out of its box and put it in this. Trust me, you will thank me later."

She flew to the chest containing the loose gemstones, handing me another drawstring sack, this one teal velvet. “Can you open the chest, please?”

I did so, looking at her with curiosity. She flew inside and began handing me stones to put in the bag. Once the first was filled she handed me another and began rummaging.

“Are you particularly attached to any of this jewelry?”

Shaking my head, I told her I wasn't. “I literally just learned they existed, and while they were a gift from the father I will never know, I assume he sent them here for a reason other than for me to play with.”

She nodded, continuing to dig. “You're pretty smart. We may travel through areas where gifts are required for safe passage. It is also a good idea to keep them on hand to use as tokens of goodwill. Many of the fairy kin in the realms love pretty, shiny things, and will be quick to join your plight if you offer them something.”

“I can't imagine anyone wouldn't want to help if the dark mage is as terrible as they say she is, but you grab whatever you think we need.”

She continued handing out items as she mumbled to herself, seeming to go through some sort of mental checklist. “Something a bit larger for the dragons...”

“I'm sorry, did you just say dragons?” I might have grown up on Earth, but we had all read the fairy tales about dragons. Huge, fire breathing creatures that could swallow a person in one gulp. Dark magic scared me, but the thought of being swallowed alive or roasted like a marshmallow absolutely terrified me. Perhaps I should just hang out here instead.

“Yes. They were on the verge of extinction even back in my day, but there was a small, very secretive clan who lived not far from the king's castle. If they still exist and we can woo them to help us, their assistance will be priceless.”

“What if we find them and they just eat us instead?” I literally shook with fear as I voiced my concern to her.

She just shook her head as she pawed through the jewelry in the chest. “Nah, unless you give them reason to believe you might taste good, you'll be fine.”

“What?” I could barely squeak out the single word.

She finally paused in her digging, and looked up at me, laughing when she got a look at my expression. “Are you truly afraid of dragons?”

“I happen to have a healthy fear of ALL creatures who can eat me as a snack.”

Shaking her head, she laughed her chiming peals of laughter as she returned to her search. “Do not fear, Princess, for we shall protect you.”

Chapter Five

She handed me the last of her choices to take as bribes, or gifts, or whatever need we had of them, and looked around one last time. I took a final glance as well, thinking I couldn't wait for a calmer time in my life, so I could return to this room and go through all the things my father had left me. There were so many crates and chests we had yet to open.

As we left the vault, I chose to use my hand print to seal the door once more. We were going to be away for an undetermined amount of time, and I felt better knowing the door would be locked while I wasn't around.

I could hear the guys in the study, so we headed that direction. Each of them had an impressive set of weapons strapped to them, and I whistled at their choices.

"I just need to change, then if one of you could help me with the sheaths for my daggers I would appreciate it."

They both nodded their assent, and I turned to head out the door.

"Oh, and would one of you grab some snacks and throw them in my pack?" That set them laughing and I huffed at them. "Well, remember, nobody wants me to get hangry."

"Don't worry, Ev. We'll be sure to feed you." Taryk smiled at me and followed me out of the study.

As we neared my bedroom door, he had a few words of advice for me. "Wear the most durable clothes you have. Leather is good, and boots if you have them. You want to get as much protection as possible from them, and either Xavier or I will help you spell them for extra strength."

I nodded, wondering what the cabin would have in store for me, knowing it would provide me with appropriate gear. I opened the closet and was not disappointed. Leather pants, which I prayed were comfortable, knee-high leather booths with a sturdy heel, both in black, and a snug fitting gray shirt. There was a black leather jacket to go over.

Lying on the bed was a black backpack, and I swapped out the one I had intended to take for what the cabin suggested. Magic knows best.

I was attempting to wiggle my way into the unreasonably tight leather pants when I heard Taryk shout from the other room. "Hey, guys, we have company!"

I tugged the T-shirt over my head as I ran out the door to see what he meant. A quick glance through the front window and I immediately saw the problem.

The malevolent mist had returned, and it looked angry. Instead of the gray tones it had always appeared in before, this time it resembled a solid black cloud. It surrounded us on all sides, pressed against the wards from every angle. I couldn't even see the forest. This was not good. Not good at all.

“I am going to finish dressing. We need to figure out what to do. Let's get Xavier after you grab my snacks.”

I returned to my room, throwing on the jacket and backpack before settling on the edge of the bed to don my footwear. Thankfully they were not as tight as the pants. Which, by the way, were very comfortable once I got them on. Even the sheathes for my daggers went on with very little fight.

Just as I was lacing up my boots, and shrill sound echoed through the cabin. Startled, I ran for the hall. Taryk came running from the kitchen, and I could hear Xavier and Celeste yelling for us.

“Hurry, get in here!” Xavier held the door and motioned for us to get inside. “Everleigh, say the words *conservatam agnovimus* quickly!”

As I followed his commands, he began leading us down the tunnel to the training room. “What is going on?” I had no clue, but there was no way it could be good if everybody was panicking.

Celeste looked more worried than I had ever seen her. “The cabin's wards have been breached. We must get out of here right now!”

“What? How? And where are we going?” I had assumed the wards were unbreakable.

“You need to create a portal to the chateau in Myntas. Quickly.” Celeste motioned toward the wall of the cave as Yuri fluttered next to her.

“I can't! I've never been there before! I don't know how!” I began to freak out. Everybody was counting on me to get them out of here, but I didn't know where to take them.

Xavier grabbed my hand as the shrieking increased. It felt as if the mountain itself was trembling. “We must hurry, the spell you cast was an instruction for the cabin to activate its self-preservation mode. We need to get out of here before it is complete. The cabin will cease to exist, and all that will be left is the study, the training room, and the tunnel leading between them. locked deep within the mountain.”

“What?” I had started repeating myself, and I could hear it, but seemed to have lost the majority of my vocabulary with the stress of the situation.

“You need to make a portal. Use our bond and see the vision I am sending to you. Take us there. Quickly.” Xavier pushed the image of a room into my mind.

The first portal I created was useless. Barely a foot across, nobody would be getting through it but Yuri. I could feel the impending disaster and my new found skills were suffering because I couldn't focus.

Taryk grabbed me by the shoulders and looked in my eyes. “You can do this. Take a deep breath, and concentrate. I am right here with you."

Willing my body to calm, I took the deep breath he suggested. The trembling in my hands slowed, and I took a moment to feel the power of the ring.

The air shimmered and the portal appeared, as I struggled to hold it long enough for everyone to make it to the other side.

Xavier poked his head through, then beckoned us to follow. It took every ounce of concentration I had to hold it open and shuffle toward it. Recognizing my struggle, Taryk picked me up and carried me through. Just as the portal snapped closed, we heard an unearthly bellow from the other side.

"What was that?" I was terrified we had just left some magical monster to terrorize Earth.

"Frustration," Celeste replied. "When we activated the preservation spell of the cabin, not only did the cabin disappear, most likely before anything had even been able to get inside, but the spell itself is set up to expel whatever magical being is in the area back to where it came from."

Sighing in relief, I posed my next question. "So, where are we exactly?"

"Illuminaire." Taryk called forth a globe of light, and I looked around curiously. We were in a room in a castle, but there were no identifying pieces showcased here.

"Let's keep the light low in case someone notices the light in a long-abandoned window. This is my old room in my father's original castle. The few times we did come to visit, we got to pick out our room and claim it. The wards placed on the castle have not been broken in all these years, and we are the only ones to have set foot in here in centuries."

Taryk lowered the globe to the floor and reduced the light to the minimum we could get by with. The still air and hush of silence unnerved me, but I was oddly excited to see the castle where my father had lived, and where he and my mother had fallen in love, if only for a few ill-fated weeks.

It looked as if it's people had just left the room. The lack of dust and grime surprised me, for a place that had essentially been abandoned for centuries.

Yuri flitted to the window, looking out. It looked to be just past dusk here, and I could barely see the darkened trees surrounding the castle.

"Do you think your family is still out there?" I asked her quietly.

"I hope so. It has been so long since I saw these woods last. Back before I was sent to you, the woods were alight with our luminescence at night. It looked as if tiny stars floated through the forest."

There was silence all around. I saw no moving creatures and heard no sounds. Not even the rustling of the wind. Whether because of the wards encompassing the castle, or some other cause, it was oddly still.

Celeste manifested and looked around. "I think we need to carry on. It would have been best to go to the chateau first so Everleigh could inherit her full powers. Since we are here, however, I believe we should get what we came for, and continue on our way. We are in danger, even if the castle is protected."

I agreed with her fully, even if it meant not spending much time here. I hoped one day I would be able to come back and see it restored to its former glory. Including my brother sitting on his throne.

Everyone nodded their agreement, and I motioned for Xavier to lead the way. In spite of its age, the heavy wooden door opened smoothly, and Xavier stepped into the dark hall and looked both ways before beckoning to the rest of us.

"It's empty, as I expected. Come on out."

As we stepped out of the bedroom, I noticed it wasn't a hall at all, but more of an open balcony. Four tall arched doorways, all matching the one we had just exited, led off this particular landing, plus a hall at either end. A grand staircase led down on both sides.

The height of the ceiling stretched high above us, and beautiful tapestries, each depicting a different scene, hung along the gray stone walls. I found myself wishing for more light, as I squinted to make out the details hidden in the gloom.

Xavier headed for one of the staircases, leading us down. "All four of us kids chose one of the bedrooms on this landing. The room we are descending into is a sitting room. We must keep the light low, as it has floor to ceiling windows facing the gardens. Nobody should be able to see, but I'd rather be safe than sorry. I cannot remember if the wards prevented people from seeing in, or just getting in."

I ran my hand along the smooth banister and marveled at how stunning it was. I could tell it was dark wood, but there wasn't enough light for more specific identification. It was obvious that the finish of the wood was high gloss, as it threw the reflection from Taryk's orb back onto the stairway.

Our footsteps echoed through the silence. As we reached the lower level, I could see the furniture sitting in place as if waiting for the family to come home. Again, I felt a rush of sadness at the thought of it here, abandoned for all this time. I made a silent vow that it would be restored to its original grandeur. Filled with family, and the sounds of little feet pattering through its great halls.

Xavier led us toward the massive fireplace at the end of the room, flanked by doors even taller than the ones leading from the bedchambers upstairs. These sat open, waiting for us to pass through. We skirted a massive table to follow along the back wall.

"This is the dining hall. The kitchen is straight ahead of us, but we won't be going through there right now."

My stomach must have ears, because it took that moment to protest loudly at its emptiness. Everybody laughed, forgetting for a moment that we were attempting to be quiet.

"Sorry. Making a portal made me hungry, I guess." I just shrugged. They should be used to this by now.

"*Everything* makes you hungry," Xavier teased.

Taryk reached into his pocket, producing a granola bar. “This will hopefully tide you over until we can sit and eat. I think we should wait till we get below where there are no windows for spies to peek into.”

Grinning, I snatched it from his hand. “You're the best,” I mumbled through the crumbs of my first taste. It was gone in four bites, and I stuffed the wrapper into my pocket. It didn't last nearly long enough, if you asked me, but my stomach was appeased.

We passed through a doorway on our left, leading into a darker, more enclosed hallway. Taryk turned up the brightness of his sphere, showing us a fairly conventional walkway with no adornments on the walls. It had high ceilings, but not soaring to match the room we just came from.

“At the end of this hallway is a set of stairs leading into the cellars. Once we enter the stairway, we can turn the light up, and be slightly less cautious about sound. As always, though, we want to be on alert constantly, just in case.”

Our footsteps echoed as we traveled the stone floors, and even our whispers seemed to bounce back at us. The whole place just seemed so lonely. I could almost feel it missing its former occupants.

The group began descending the flight of steps ahead of me. I couldn't seem to stop pausing to look around, even when there wasn't much to see. As soon as I got both feet onto the stairs, I felt a firm nudge from behind.

I made a squeak as I attempted to keep my balance, as there was no railing to grab on to. Taryk spun around and caught my arm as I pinwheeled; as soon as I felt certain I wasn't going to go crashing down, I turned around. Nothing but emptiness greeted me.

“Something pushed me!”

Taryk brushed past me to return to the hallway, searching for what or who might have given me the extra “help” onto the steps. He didn't discover anything more than I had.

“Walk between Xavier and I. As a matter of fact, hold my hand.”

I smirked at him. “Aw, you want to hold my hand?”

Eyebrow cocked, he held his out. “Safety first. Besides, how do we know you didn't make that up just so you could ask to hold my hand?”

Snorting with derision, I put my hand on my hip. “Why Taryk, are you calling me a liar?”

“If the shoe fits...”

He was lucky I didn't have anything to throw at him in that moment. Yuri, who had been very quiet since we arrived, spoke up from the hood of my jacket where she had been riding.

“I'll watch your back. I'm in the perfect position to do so,” she offered. “We need to keep on moving.”

I thanked her, and threaded my fingers through Taryk's, refusing to admit that I might be enjoying this as more than a way to keep me from tumbling ass over teakettle to the stone floor below. The stairs curved in a wide spiral, making it difficult to see ahead of or behind us very far.

Twice we passed doorways leading onto floors. The first one Xavier ignored. He began to turn off onto the second, but Yuri halted him.

"Not this one. The very bottom."

Xavier looked at her, his face showing his surprise. "The dungeons?"

Yuri nodded. "Yes. He wanted to be certain that even if the castle crumbled, the room would be protected deep below the surface."

Xavier paused, and the rest of us came to a stop behind him. "We need to think over our game plan very carefully. The dungeons are located far below this level. I am unsure if the original spell placed on the castle was extended to them. They are warded to keep out intruders, obviously, but I am unsure if they have the same protections."

I was confused. "Well, if the castle is undisturbed, and you have to go through the castle to get to the dungeon, then should the dungeons not be safe also?"

Yuri piped up before Xavier managed to. "There is a tunnel leading from the dungeons to a place deep within our forest. Heavily protected, at least it used to be, but it is open to the world outside of the castle. Out fiercest warriors used to guard it."

"Nobody wanted to drag prisoners, who were often screaming and fighting, through the castle itself. So they were brought in through the tunnel. It's also far enough down that nobody from the castle above would be wandering in to it accidentally." Xavier looked thoughtful as he contemplated our next move.

"Well, whether it has the same protections or not, that's irrelevant at this point. We need to get down there. At least we know now that we need to be extra cautious." I didn't have a whole lot of patience for standing in this stairwell as we debated the subject.

"You have a point. Let's move. Stay close to each other; let's be as quiet as we can. I hope we can find this hidden room without too much trouble.

The longer we climbed down the steps, the more I wondered just how far we needed to go. I had been able to tell by looking out the window that the castle was set on a steep hillside, although not quite what I would call a cliff. The forest surrounded it on all sides, so the tunnel could lead any direction.

Eventually, we reached a small landing. Our way into what I assumed was the dungeon stood blocked by a massive door fashioned out of a solid piece of timber. A small window was cut in the middle of the door. Four metal bars blocked the possibility of anything getting through, and it was covered by a metal looking plate on the opposite side.

We had no way to see what awaited us when we opened that door. If our luck held, the answer would be nothing, remaining abandoned as it had been meant to be. If luck was not on our side, it could be any number of disastrous situations. I crossed my fingers and hoped for the best.

Chapter Six

Yuri left the comfort of my hood and flew to the front of the group. “You get the door open, and let me do a little scouting. I am the smallest and the fastest.”

I wanted to protest, but knew she spoke the truth. “We'll keep the door cracked. If you see anything at all that looks suspicious, come right back here so we can decide how to deal with it, okay?”

Before she could answer, Celeste spoke up. “Ah, but I am invisible. I can slip through the hall unseen.”

We all looked at each other, Taryk and Xavier shrugging. I just waved my hand at her. “Go. Let us know what you find.”

Yuri returned to my hood, huffing with indignation when she plopped down. “How am I going to be of assistance if you won't let me do anything to help?"

"You will have your jobs, as we each shall have ours. It is in the best interest of the entire group that we let the person best suited for the job actually do it. Don't worry, you will get your opportunities."

We stood in silence after that, waiting for Celeste to return. I shifted from foot to foot, impatient and anxious at the same time, hoping and praying that the dungeon was empty.

After what felt like forever, but was probably only minutes, she returned, and manifested in the midst of us. Since we had a forged a bond, I felt her presence before she appeared, but everyone else was startled.

"I did not search every cell, but I traversed the hallway down to the other door at the far end and saw no signs of trouble. It is dark, and we will need quite a bit of light to function."

"Okay, let's move in." Xavier opened the heavy door the rest of the way, and we filed in behind him cautiously.

Taryk positioned his globe of light near the ceiling, turning up the brightness so we could easily see around us. The floor here in the hall was packed dirt instead of stone to match the walls. Doors were positioned on each side of the corridor, somewhat irregularly and rather far apart.

The first of the cell doors stood open, and I took the opportunity to peek inside. The room was nothing more than a rectangle with solid stone walls and floor. No bed, or creature comforts provided.

"People were actually kept in here?" I felt horrified. Once the door was closed there would be no light, and you would experience total isolation and sensory deprivation.

"All manner of creatures have resided in these cells. They are both physically and magically reinforced to ensure there can be no escape, and no attacks could come from within them." Yuri flitted around, having left my hood to join in the investigation. "The walls between them are thick to help guarantee there can be no communication between the prisoners."

In spite of knowing that one must do truly atrocious things on the outside to make it in here, I still felt bad for anyone subjected to it. Until I thought about the dark mage and her injustices. She belonged in a place far worse than this, so...

"The entrance to your hidden room will be in a space between the cells. Your father would not tell me which one, to protect the location should I be compromised, but he said you will feel it." Yuri seemed more distressed than the rest of us at this point, and I had no idea how to calm her.

"Well, then I will just start making my way down the row and see what happens. The rest of you can keep an eye out just in case."

Stopping at the first expanse of wall, I stood and waited to see if there was any indication that this might be the one. Nothing seemed to pique my attention, so I moved on. One by one, I paused in front the bare expanses of wall between the cell doors. I crisscrossed the wide walkway since the cell doors were offset from each other. I made it to the heavy door at the end of the cell block having found nothing.

"What is on the other side of this door? Are there more cells?" I paused in front of it, hoping whatever might be over there wouldn't be as terrible as my imagination started forming. But I hadn't found anything in this particular area, so we needed to move forward.

Xavier walked up and stood next to me. "There are just a few in there. They were reserved for the worst of the worst."

"All right, let's check them out." I reached to push the door open and received multiple cries of "Wait!" in unison.

"Let me go first." Celeste reappeared next to me. "I only came as far as this door, and we need to be certain it's safe."

I assumed that if something had been in there, we would know it by now. Near the top of the door was a tiny, barred window leading directly through to the other side, and we hadn't exactly been quiet. But I hung back and waited for her to investigate.

She was gone only briefly. "Everleigh, on the other side of this door is very unpleasant. The room was used for torture, and there are souls still trapped here. You will no doubt be able to feel them, and I do not want you to enter unprepared. I don't believe they will be able to physically harm you, but you will be uncomfortable. On the plus side, I did not detect any with their magic intact, either."

"Can I release them and send them on their way?" If we could purge them from the area, it would be much easier for me to work. And seeing as how I was unsure whether trapped souls could communicate, I didn't want to leave any witnesses to our escapades. Especially since I assumed we most likely would not be able to bring all the things from the hidden room with us.

Celeste looked thoughtful. “I cannot say. Since you have not performed your invocation, you are not technically the reigning scribe. However, you are very powerful, and may be able to. I can show you how.”

“Wait a minute!” Taryk broke in. “We don't need to spend the extra time worrying about them. Let's just get in, get what we need, and get out.”

I took his hand and explained to him why I didn't want to leave them in there if we didn't have to.

“As much as I hate to admit it, she is right.” Xavier looked concerned at the prospect of leaving behind any tattletales. “But we also have to consider that using magic here is like sending up a beacon. If there is anyone monitoring, they will know someone is in the castle.”

“Releasing a soul actually uses very little magic,” Celeste explained. “It is similar to opening a portal, but because the veil is everywhere, it is a short distance to travel. She basically just needs to open it up and it will suck them through.”

“Well, let's get started. Show me how to do it, please. The sooner they are gone, the sooner we can get on with our search.”

I released Taryk to place my palms against Celeste's outstretched, spectral hands. “I am going to attempt to use the bond to show you how to open a portal to the veil. Hopefully, you will be successful. Once open, the veil will seek to balance and pull the souls through to where they belong. It requires a great sacrifice of energy, especially the first few times, so be prepared.”

I nodded grimly, and closed my eyes, saying a quick prayer that this would work, and I would be able to complete the task. Our bond proved to be strong, indeed, and it took only seconds for me to receive the information she attempted to show me. She pushed it forth, and I allowed it to settle in, committing to memory not only the procedure, but the feelings and thoughts she experienced throughout the process.

It seemed both simple and complex at the same time. Provided the universe would allow me to generate a portal through the veil without the invocation, I believed I could manage the task.

“Is there anything else I should know?” Heads shook all the way around, and I prepared to enter the chamber of horrors, as I had begun thinking of it. “Wait!”

Everybody turned to look at me.

“What?” Taryk had grasped my hand again and squeezed it tightly.

“Celeste? You are a soul. Won't it try to suck you through as well?” I was panicking at the mere thought of losing her, especially by my own hand.

She paused. “I suppose you are correct. Good catch.” Looking pensive, she frowned as she tried to decide the best course of action.

“How about if I give the bracelet to Xavier, and you two go down the hall, and on the other side of the far doorway. Taryk can come with me for moral support. You guys can wait in the stairwell for us to finish.”

“And I should do what, exactly?” Yuri piped up from her place in my hood.

I slid the bracelet off and passed it to Xavier as I answered. “I will leave that up to you. I know your people have an affinity for souls. What I don't know enough about is how this may affect you, so I don't want to make any decisions for you.”

My response seemed to curtail any sass she had been about to give me, and she hovered quietly, deep in thought for a moment. Her tiny eyebrows drew together as she debated her options.

“I believe I will wait for you on this side of the door. Close enough to be of assistance as needed, but not directly in the thick of things.”

Nodding, I turned to the door and prepared to open it. Xavier laid his hand on my shoulder one last time before heading down the hall with Celeste.

“I don't know how many souls are in there, or how strong they are. But if you need help keeping them out, open our bond, and allow me to assist you in any way I can.”

I let go of Taryk to hug him and nodded. “Go. I will not open this door until the other is closed.”

Listening to his footsteps echo as they retreated gave me a chill. I had never before been subject to anything like I was about to experience, and I knew I advanced into it ill prepared. For a soul to be tortured, and then trapped in the place it had happened must be maddening.

As the door latched on the other end of the hallway, I looked Taryk in the eyes and took a deep breath, placing my hand on the door once more.

“Remember, whatever you are feeling when you enter, it isn't real. I will not let them hurt you. What you are about to feel is only the echo of actions past."

I nodded, swallowing to wet my suddenly parched mouth. It was game time.

I pushed the door open and stepped through. Taryk's orb lit up most of the room, leaving few dark corners, and my eyes widened in shock.

The ceiling was high with chains hanging down. Numerous tables and racks stood throughout the space. A deep pit went directly through the floor in the center of the room. Manacles with more chains hung from the walls. Dark stains marred most of the surfaces. The air in the room was sluggish. It stank of mold and had the coppery tang of old blood.

The doors to the few cells leading off the room were closed, and my imagination began to run away with me, imagining what it must have been like to wait in one. You would easily be able to hear the screams of those who were here in the foyer, and quite probably the sounds of whatever torture was being administrated at the time.

I looked at Taryk, who squeezed my hand for reassurance. I was wary as I had not felt any souls within the confines of the room, and did not know whether I should attempt to open the portal or wait. I feared using my voice and attracting unwanted attention.

About the time I won the argument with myself about opening the portal, whether I felt the souls or not, they made themselves known. They slammed into my psyche like a ton of bricks, and I staggered; even Taryk's grip on my hand was not enough to keep me from slamming into the wall.

I had not been prepared, and once they struck, I couldn't erect a shield. My brain couldn't even comprehend what they had endured. It felt like rusty nails dragging along the inside of my skull. I could hear their screams and feel their pain. Tears coursed down my face, and I instinctively curled into the tiniest ball I could make of myself, trying to protect against the onslaught.

My bones felt as if they were being broken. My flesh burned as if someone dropped acid onto my skin, I could feel it eating through the layers. Their anger at being confined here was all consuming. I didn't know how much more I could take without breaking.

It took Xavier reaching through our bond and shutting everything out for me to get hold of myself again. Once I managed that, I looked around, realizing we were no longer in the torture chamber. Blinking, I looked up at the worried faces surrounding me.

"Thank goodness you came back to us." Celeste hovered nervously above me.

"What happened?" Taryk knelt on the floor next to me, half cradling me in his lap.

Instead of answering them right away, I inspected myself. I saw no blood, no patches of flesh that had been eaten away. My bones all felt intact, even the arm that had slammed into the wall was only sore. My head though, that was another issue entirely. I would never forget what I just experienced. Ever.

Gingerly, I stood and looked at the others. "That. Was. Terrifying."

Taryk still held my hand, having gotten up beside me. "Can you tell us what happened? If you don't want to talk about it, show me through our bond."

"I hope nobody ever has to see that. Don't go looking for it. I am going to do my best to lock it away and pretend it never happened."

"Do you think that's healthy?" Xavier started to give me his opinion, and I cut him off sharply.

"Just. Don't. Okay? Don't."

I took a deep breath and looked at Celeste. She waited patiently for me to begin.

"I was inadequately prepared. I got caught off guard because I couldn't feel them at first. I couldn't feel anything."

She nodded. "I believe they linger deep within the pit. I apologize, it didn't occur to me to let you know you may have to scan for them."

"Don't apologize, it's not your fault. Whoever tortured these poor souls is at fault. I don't care what they did, nobody deserves this. Nobody."

The group stood quietly for a moment at the vehemence of my words.

Yuri fluttered next to me. "*Nobody* is a strong statement. You have no idea what they may have done. All creatures are capable of doing horrific things."

"I don't care. If you could feel the pain. The anguish. It's wanting to die but knowing the suffering will continue. There is NO REASON to *ever* subject any living thing to what just invaded my head. EVER."

I was breathing erratically by the time I had finished the statement, and my heart was hammering. I had slipped back to the very edge of my control just thinking about it. Taryk squeezed my hand gently, trying to pull me back.

“Not even the dark mage?” Xavier asked quietly, looking me square in the eye. “If I gave you some of the details of what she did, maybe you would change your mind.”

His quiet statement punctured the cloud surrounding my thoughts. The soft voice with which he delivered those two sentences spoke loud and clear.

I took a deep breath. Then another. I reached out for Taryk's calm presence, desperately attempting to match my rhythms to his. He reached out and enveloped me in the calm that was his way, and my body responded.

I looked at Xavier. “I'm sorry. I just needed to get control so I can go back in and get rid of them.”

“Is there another way?” Taryk made it painfully obvious that he didn't want to see me go through that again if he didn't have to.

“No. There isn't. And I will be fine, now that I know what to expect. I have a plan.” I looked at him and winked.

“Oh boy...” Yuri teased me. “Look out. She *has a plan*!” She zipped toward the ceiling as I swatted at her playfully.

“Quiet, you. Or I shall take you in there with me.” She ducked behind Xavier, who was shaking with silent laughter.

“Okay, guys, here's my idea.”

Chapter Seven

Taking a deep breath, I rested my hand against the wood door, the only thing separating me from the chaos waiting on the other side. The genius of my plan lay in its simplicity.

Xavier would use our bond to create a mental shield for me. As soon as Taryk and I stepped through the door, I would call forth the portal. A merge between the two of us would allow me to access and use his power if I had trouble keeping the portal open while it sucked the tortured souls through. Once all the nasty beasties had made their way to the other side, I'd close the portal, and we move on with our search. Easy, right?

Ha. Since when did anything ever go as planned?

I took one last look at Taryk, and he nodded at me, smiled, and squeezed my hand. “You can do this.”

I nodded back, pushed the door open and stepped inside. Immediately, I felt the pressure from the agonized souls as they attempted to get inside my head once more. Xavier held strong though, and pressure was the only effect they had on me this time.

Calling for the ring to guide and assist me, I made my first attempt at opening a portal to the veil. It opened, wavered, and disappeared. Frustrated, I dug deep, and tried again. This time I succeeded in opening a portal approximately three feet across. The view to the other side entranced me, and I lost concentration, allowing it to slam shut once more.

“Damn it.”

Taryk squeezed my hand. “Once it is open, draw on me. Look at the floor. You've got this.”

I nodded. Third time's a charm, yes? My energy had already begun to wane, so it was a good thing I had him to rely on.

Squaring my shoulders, I requested the portal again. This time, I took his advice and did not look to the other side. It almost got me when I realized I could see the souls as they passed through, but I was able to catch myself and refocus.

We had made it until the last soul. He was a great big one and fighting every step of the way. I struggled to maintain the portal while I waited for him to succumb to its call. All of a sudden, I felt Taryk's hand tighten on my own. Turning to look toward him, I saw my worst fear.

Celeste, clearly discernible, had been dragged down the hallway and into the chamber. Doors were no use in holding her spiritual form. You could see her struggle to resist the call of the veil, but it was proving to be too much for her. Bile rose in my throat. I could not lose her. She caught my eye and began shaking her head furiously.

"He must pass over. DO NOT close it until he is gone!" She continued to fight, as did the massive creature we were trying to banish. She would occasionally gain some ground, backing farther away, whereas he kept inching closer. She came within a few feet of the portal, then appeared to get a grip and stopped short.

I pulled everything I could get my hands on from Taryk, but I knew his power waned as well. I began to fear we were going to lose this fight when a beacon of light shot across the room. Yuri, in all her golden glory appeared to fly right up to the monster and shove him through.

The second he was gone, I released the energy and the portal appeared to close in upon itself. Taryk dragged us back into the hall and we sagged against the wall, with Yuri and Celeste on our heels.

"Yuri! My hero. How did you do that?" I had never been so thankful for my little friend as I was that moment.

Xavier came striding down the hall to join us, having released the block as soon as the pressure to get in my head disappeared. "Are you okay? You did it."

I shook my head. "I am exhausted, but Yuri did it. She shoved the last one through, and saved Celeste too."

Xavier looked taken aback. "Celeste needed saving?"

"I am eternally grateful I am bound to the bracelet. We just discovered exactly how far I can travel from it, no matter what the circumstance. I could feel the portal trying to drag me across, but my tie to the bracelet won the fight. I could not move one more inch away from it."

"Celeste was only a few feet from the portal, and I had one giant butthead refusing to cross. About the time I started to wonder if he was stronger than the call of the veil, Yuri came in and pushed him through. How did you do it?" I turned to look at her.

She smiled. "My family has always had the ability to manipulate loose souls in a small way. Occasionally, we would run across wanderers who simply needed help. We did what we could to assist them to cross. I wasn't sure if I would be able to force one who didn't want to go, but because the veil was already calling to him, I just helped it along."

I sank to the dirt floor. "I need to rest and eat something before we do any more searching. I'm sure Taryk does too."

We all agreed a break was in order, and nobody wanted to take it on the other side of the door. Taryk rummaged around in his pack and brought out sandwiches and waters for each of us. I shared with Yuri, who had come to rest on my knee.

We attempted to make small talk around bites of our sandwiches. Somehow, we all wanted to pretend we weren't eating on a dirty floor, directly outside the door of a torture chamber, as we searched for items in preparation for a war that would change our lives forever.

I wanted nothing more than to curl up right here and take a nap, torture chamber right next door or not. But naps were a luxury I could no longer afford. Sighing, I finished the last of my sandwich and got to my feet. Time to resume our search.

We filed through the door silently. I hesitated briefly, waiting for the barrage of pain and terror that had besieged me before. Thankfully nothing came. I took a few more steps into the room and paused, waiting to see if anything jumped out at me. Nothing did, so I moved to the area on my right, intending to work my way counterclockwise through the room.

As I did so, I asked Xavier questions. "What is that pit for, and where does it lead to?

He shook his head. "We were told it goes on forever, not that we ever tried to find out. It was used for disposal, mostly. We didn't get involved in this much, since we were just kids. We weren't actually allowed down here, for obvious reasons."

I knew better than to ask him disposal for what. At the wall between the second and third door, I hit pay dirt. The closer I got to it, the stronger the call became.

"This is it, you guys." I couldn't help but be excited that what we were looking for actually existed. Part of me had been afraid we were on a wild goose chase. They hurried over to stand by my side.

I looked at Yuri. "Do you know how I am supposed to get in?"

She nodded. "Place both hands against the stones, palms open, fingers spread wide."

Following her instructions, I did exactly as she described. For good measure, I leaned against the wall, placing my forehead against the cool stones. I tried not to think about the horrors this particular wall had seen. It was only seconds before I heard a cracking sounds and felt the wall tremble. I stepped back, and we all waited with breaths held.

A section of wall shifted outward slightly, splitting in two along the mortar lines, then sliding to the side. The alcove revealed was not large. The shelf created out of the stone wall itself held three items, and a parchment with both the soul scribe crest and the one I assumed to be my father's imprinted on it in a wax seal.

Reaching out, I took the scroll into my hands. As I did, the crest began to glow, and melted away. Unrolling it, I took in my father's handwriting once more, and read his message out loud.

My darling daughter,

If you have made it this far in your journey, I want you to know how proud I am of you already. The items you see before you are the only ones with the undisputed capability of defeating the dark mage. They were created from her own blood, collected at the time she was first imprisoned.

The pendant has been spelled to reflect her magic. If you are wearing it, her spells will be reversed, reflecting back on her instead.

The potion will temporarily null her magic. It must get on her skin. Even a single drop will have the intended effect. The vial is protected to be unbreakable, so you must remove the stopper to make use of it.

Lastly, the dagger you see here will end her life. As the smith forged it in his fires, her own spelled blood was worked into the blade. Not only is it a spell that will turn her own blood to poison within her body once her skin has been pierced, the dagger will be drawn to her. The blood within the weapon will search out her body, as the blood within desires to be reunited with its origins. In hand-to-hand combat, you will be guided to the best strike. Should you have to throw it, it's aim will be true.

You may also choose to bond the dagger to yourself. A single drop of your blood, and should you lose possession of it, it will return to your hand if you should call for it.

Guard these items with everything you have available. I have no doubt she will continue to grow in power through the years, and you will need all the assistance you can get.

I have faith in you. Go forth and prevail. Save the realms from her evil.

He did not sign the letter. I stared at the items on the shelf in awe. Reaching out, I picked up the pendant first. The disc was hollow and filled with a dark, viscous liquid. I hoped it had been filled with a concoction other than her actual blood.

The vial of potion was not large, and the liquid inside reminded me of green water, thin and translucent. I tucked it into one of the small pockets on my jacket that had a zipper.

Lastly, I picked up the dagger, pulling it from its sheath. It had been created from dark, monotone metal. The satin finish picked up the light, but there were no adornments. Compared to the pair I wore in my thigh holsters, this seemed bland and innocuous enough. I could feel the power within when I held it though, proving that things were not always what they seemed.

In spite of my aversion to spilling my own blood, even a drop, I knew the best choice was to perform the ritual to bind it to me. I didn't believe it would prevent anyone else from using it, and I wanted to be sure I could always retrieve it, should the need arise.

Holding it in my right hand, I quickly pricked my left thumb. Touching the dagger to the scarlet drop welling against my pale skin caused an instant response. The metal blade heated and sucked the drop of blood into itself. Following the contact it cooled immediately and I returned it to it's sheath.

Taryk helped me affix this newest weapon to my belt, beside my daggers, and I looked at my group. We had made it through this portion of our journey. We successfully collected the items my father had hidden here for me.

“Well, I believe we can consider this mission a success. Is there anything else we can think of that should be done here before we move on?”

Everyone shook their heads, except for Yuri, who flew to the forefront of the group.

“I have a suggestion, if I may?”

"Of course, Yuri. What do you have in mind?"

She flitted to and fro for a moment before speaking. "I believe we should consider making contact with my people, if they are still here. They will have valuable information about what surrounds the castle, and whether the dragons are still in existence here. If we are to return here for war, it would be in our best interest to begin preparing as soon as possible."

Immediately the others protested, talking over one another in their haste to explain why this idea could not happen.

"STOP!" Throwing my hands up, I waited for each of them to calm down and quit running their mouths. "Yuri is right. We are going to need all the help we can get."

Celeste weighed in first. "You should not leave the castle. Until you perform your invocation you are vulnerable. You have no heiress, and we cannot risk the scribe magic being released and then hijacked by the dark mage."

The others readily nodded at her assessment, but Yuri broke in.

"I have a solution. As I mentioned before, this tunnel leads into the forest, directly to the heart of our territory. I suggest that I go and see what happens. Our warriors, if they are still on guard, may be ill-prepared if a group comes wandering out the tunnel which hasn't been used in centuries. Once I make contact, there will be two choices. Either I return to you, and we travel together to the safety of my homeland, or I return with a delegation of my people to the tunnel, and therefore the castle."

As much as I didn't want to send her out there all by herself, I knew that if anyone were to go, it should be her, and that none of us could risk leaving the castle. Logistics just needed to be figured out before she left.

“What about the wards? Will she be able to return via the tunnel? I should not go out, but I am reluctant to bring anyone in either. Yuri, you have not been home in well over a century. How will you know which of your people are trustworthy?”

“I am royalty. Our people cannot betray me, no matter how long I have been gone.” She looked absolutely certain.

“But what if they have been possessed? What of the dark mage has some sort of magical hold on them? I know that sort of thing is possible.” I was terrified to have made this leg of the journey successfully, and then have it end in disaster because we trusted the wrong people.

Xavier held up his hand. “When she returns, I will meet her at the place in the tunnel where the wards end. I will remain within the confines of the ward while I assess those with her. As she is royalty to her people, I am such to all this realm. I will be able to read their intentions. If they are safe, I will bring them to you. If they are not, I will help Yuri back into the ward and we will return to you alone. Then we can make decisions about what to do next.”

I took a deep breath. “Unless you choose not to return, Yuri. I do not hold you responsible for any more of my journey. While I would love to have you, I imagine you must yearn to return to your people and your life here.” I chewed the inside of my cheek, tasting blood, as I waited for her response. I'd grown pretty attached to her in a very short while.

She flew right up to my face, poking my nose with her tiny finger once again. “You are not getting rid of me that easily. I will follow you to the ends of the realm, if I can help you in any way.” She turned to fly toward the tunnel door, then turned quickly. “That is, if you want me to. I will stay here if that is your wish.”

I couldn't help the huge grin I felt stretch across my face. “Go, do what you need to do, and get your butt back here. Pronto.”

She answered with nothing but a matching grin and flew out the door Xavier had opened for her. I managed to stand still for all of five minutes after she had left, then the pacing began.

“What should we be doing while we wait for her? Xavier what can you tell us about the subjects of this realm? Are there really dragons?”

He smiled. “There are many in this realm. Too many to cram into one lesson. Yuri's people are the wood sprites. They have been responsible for the forests in this realm since its creation. Our families were always close, and I believe they will be strong allies if the dark mage has not taken them hostage or wiped them out entirely.”

I shuddered at the thought. I'd be devastated if Yuri went in search of them only to find annihilation and ruin where her people once ruled.

“There were dragons, many generations ago. I cannot say if they still exist, or whether they still inhabit our realm. If they did, the dark mage would have done her best to enslave them. Or massacre them if she couldn't bend them to her will. Dragons are fierce warriors, and not to be trifled with or taken lightly."

Now the shudder turned to fear. As I told Yuri, if something could eat me for a snack, I was less than excited to encounter it. But I also knew we needed every ally that could be rounded up.

"There are many other species of magical being here. The land surrounding the castle used to hold a small delegation from each as ambassadors of sorts. Many of them stayed even after my parents moved into the castle closer to town. My father still returned here to meet with them regularly. I do not know what has happened since the dark mage took over." Xavier's face remained stoic, but I could hear the pain in his voice and feel his sorrow through our bond.

Taryk, having been silent for most of our conversation, looked pensive. "What is the likelihood we can gather an army, and bring them inside the castle walls for safety? I bet this castle has everything needed to maintain a small population, if we can get it going again."

I turned to him in surprise. "That's a fantastic idea." Looking at Xavier, I raised my brows. "Well, what do you think?"

"Getting it going again would not be a problem. Keeping it secret would be the biggest obstacle. I would need to read the wards to see exactly how they are set up. If they are only for keeping people from entering the area, it would draw too much attention to have signs of life begin showing up where anyone could happen along and see it."

He had a point. A castle dormant for centuries could not suddenly come to life without arousing suspicions.

"My understanding is that everything within the boundaries of the wards are suspended in time, for lack of a better explanation." He continued thinking aloud. "That's why nothing became overgrown or deteriorated in any way. If we could alter the ward to create the illusion of remaining unchanged to anyone who looked at it, we might be able to get away with it."

He took up pacing, while I returned to stand beside Taryk. I could feel him puzzling over the details in his head. We tossed ideas back and forth, working out a semblance of a plan while we waited. Celeste occasionally chimed in, but mostly floated the perimeter of the room.

Finally, she interrupted. "I'm sorry, but I believe there is something that requires your attention."

The three of us turned our attention to her, curious.

"What is it?" Taryk asked her.

Before she could tell us, Yuri called to me through our bond. "Xavier, Yuri is returning."

He nodded and exited via the wooden door leading to the tunnel. My stomach tightened into a bundle of nerves. Meeting new people had always been difficult but learning of all these magical beings and adding them to my world took it to a whole other level.

I'd gone back to pacing the room when Yuri and Xavier both sent a message along our bond. Xavier announced they were returning with a delegation. Yuri demanded I put on my tiara, and not argue with her. Her final command was to go along with the story line as they told it.

I looked at Taryk, relaying the message. He nodded to me.

"Better do it then. They probably have a reason for it."

I took off the backpack and rummaged through it, removing the bag that held the tiara. Settling it on my head, I felt a little silly. Why was I wearing a tiara with my leather outfit? I probably looked ridiculous.

Taryk looked me over. "May I?"

Before I knew what he wanted to do, my leather pants and jacket had changed just enough to look appropriate. They went from black to dark silver, and the top underneath turned to silk. The leather jacket morphed into a cloak, and even my boots got an upgrade.

He handed me a clip, and Celeste instructed me to put my hair into a bun, then replace the tiara. Speechless from the transformation Taryk had pulled off, I did as I was told without arguing. I briefly, and humorously, wished the dungeon had a mirror available, but still thought I looked pretty fantastic from the view I had.

Taryk smiled at me, and Celeste stood beaming. "It suits you, child," she declared.

Just like that, the time for adjustments had passed, because we heard voices coming down the tunnel.

Chapter Eight

"Stand still, my child," Celeste instructed me. "You are royalty here. I will clue you in through our bond if there are actions you need to take." With that last message, she winked out of sight.

I did my best to stand up straight, and "look royal" in spite of having no clue what it actually entailed. Taryk gave my hand one last squeeze as the door began to open, then stood by my side. Xavier entered first, having also adjusted his attire, followed by Yuri, who had donned a tiara herself somewhere along the line.

Trying not to look surprised, I stood motionless and waited for them to take the lead. Following Yuri were four other wood sprites, one of whom looked to be ancient.

Yuri placed herself between the other sprites and myself.

“Grandma, this is Princess Everleigh, King Oseron's only living daughter. Your Highness, our monarch, Queen Flora of the realm of Amarys.”

“Nod your head as regally as possible in her direction. To welcome her.” Celeste's voice rang softly through my head, and I did my best.

“Welcome, Queen Flora. Thank you for coming.”

Internally freaking out, I did my best to appear outwardly calm. Nobody warned me ahead of time I would have to pretend to be royalty. I hadn't prepared for this.

“My child, it is a pleasure to finally meet you. Your father apprised me of your impending birth so many years ago.”

Even her voice sounded old, and I couldn't guess at how long she had been alive. Knowing she was Yuri's grandmother gave me an extra layer of security and helped me to trust her motives for being here.

Her gentle smile put me even more at ease, and I allowed myself to relax just a smidgen. I had great hopes that we would be able to work together.

Looking into my eyes, she continued. “Your father believed that you would be the only one capable of defeating the dark mage. I, for one, believe he was right. In his day, he and I were allies, close friends and confidants. It pained me so to lose him.”

She turned, looking at Xavier next. “It brightens my heart to see two of his children are with us and have returned to their homeland.”

I looked at Xavier, unsure how to respond. He smiled at her. "We will do our best to return our lands to the glory they once held."

"The prince has told me of your wishes to gather an army here. I have both good news and bad in that regard. The good news is that you will find nearly every creature still living willing to help you on your quest to defeat her. Even better news is that she has not been seen in this realm for many years. She does still have spies to do her bidding though."

I watched her, wondering what the bad news would turn out to be. So far, this seemed to be all to simple. The path we were on couldn't possibly turn out this easily conquered.

"The bad news, my dear, is the reason she has moved on. She sucked every last drop of magic out of the land that she was able. Very few us possess any at all."

My jaw dropped. No magic? How was such a thing even possible?

The queen continued to tell the story of the dreadful years while the mage reigned supreme in this land. "Her minions captured every magical being possible. She began with those who held the most potent skills, stripping them of the power they held. Many of them perished in the process. Those who didn't, returned to their lives a shell of what they had once been."

Her telling of the tale ignited my anger once again. Suddenly, even this torture room of horrors seemed too good an end for her.

She continued on, and finished her story with the statement, "As long as no detectable magic is used here, I do not think we will cause her to pay us any attention."

How were we supposed to beat her with no magic? The few of us here could not do it alone. Despondency threatened to overtake what had been staunch optimism just moments before.

I struggled to remain standing tall when all I wanted was to sink to the floor. It felt like our quest had been dealt a death blow before it even started.

Xavier turned to me and took my hand. "Everleigh, I have a plan. You will not like this but listen through to the end."

I immediately tensed. If he had to warn me ahead of time I wouldn't like it, then I knew I would hate it.

"Celeste, may I request your presence?" He waited to continue speaking until she appeared.

She smiled serenely. "How may I be of assistance?"

The sprites had startled somewhat at her sudden appearance, but not as much as I would have had it been unexpected. I supposed when accustomed to a world full of magic, some things didn't affect you the way it did others.

"I'd like you to just confirm that my idea is viable." He began by addressing Celeste. Once she had nodded her assent, he continued on. "I'll start with the part you will like least, Ev, and go from there. I will remain here—"

"Stop. Stop right there. No. The answer is no. Absolutely not. I cannot—"

"Everleigh." Taryk took his turn to interrupt at the same time as Celeste. "Listen to him, Everleigh."

Straightening my shoulders once more, I chewed my lower lip to help hold my silence. Whether I was royalty or not, he could not entice me to agree with his crazy scheme.

He looked me right in the eye as he continued. "I *will* remain here in the castle. For a number of reasons. The main one being this: there are only two people who can cross the wards. You and me. One of us must remain in order to bring everyone in."

"Why are we even bothering with that plan? No magic means that by gathering them here we are just drawing attention that we wanted to avoid. We cannot protect them all by ourselves if she returns suspicious."

He smiled at me and continued. "You will return to Myntas and perform the invocation. Once you have reached the full height of your powers, you will return here. As a Soul Scribe, with Celeste's aid, you can reassign magic to their souls." He looked at Celeste. "That is within the powers of the reigning scribe, is it not?"

Celeste appeared deep in thought before she answered. "Yes. The universe will be seeking to correct the imbalance of magic. It is unnatural. It is difficult, however, to do on a large scale, and will take time. Everleigh is only a single person, no matter how powerful she is."

"We will begin to work on the details while you are away.

Hopefully, by the time you return, we will have a more specific plan. Queen Flora has agreed to help me." Xavier acted as if all had been agreed upon, but I still wanted to argue with him. I didn't know if I could continue on and leave him behind.

"The only other question," Celeste pondered, "is where we can get that amount of magic to distribute. Everleigh needs to be at full strength, and therefore cannot afford to spare any. The other option would be to call their own magic back to them, but that would alert the dark mage in an instant."

Queen Flora chose that moment to interject. "From the dragons, of course."

My head jerked toward her, giving her cause to chuckle. "There is nothing to fear, my child. There are only three of them left in the realm, and they are our allies. Dragons are the keepers of magic. The only beings who can share it without depleting their own."

I stared at her, still in disbelief. Dozens of questions flashed through my brain, but I managed to keep my silence while she continued to explain.

"They went deep into hiding while the magic was being sucked from the land. The mage did manage to capture a few, and in the end, each of those perished. The clan was not large to begin with, and each loss decimated their chances for survival. The dragons became unable to hatch their eggs as the magic in the realm dwindled. Something about the imbalance has a negative effect on their procreation. The remaining three took the eggs that had already been laid into hiding with them, in hopes that once the balance became restored, they could continue to develop and hatch."

In spite of being terrified of them, my heart broke for their losses. To lose your kin while being unable to add to your family must've been shattering.

"We have an emissary who occasionally visits them. I have agreed to send them to tell the dragons of our plans and ask their assistance."

Celeste used our bond to prompt me once again, and I almost jumped at the unexpected contact. "Thank her."

"I can't thank you enough. As you know, we will need all the assistance we can gather." She nodded regally in response, and I turned to Xavier.

"We will need to iron out some details before I go. Perhaps optimizing the wards should be our first step?"

I may have disagreed with his plan emotionally, but damn it, he made perfect sense. Even if I didn't want to admit it. And if we were going through with it, then we needed to get started.

Yuri announced she would see the delegation to the edge of the ward with Xavier, and then return to us. The rest of us began strategizing.

While we talked, I returned to pacing the room and waiting for the two of them to return. If I thought my stomach had been a bundle of nerves before, I was now sure I knew what it felt like to swallow live wires. I hadn't yet accepted I would be leaving without Xavier, and I didn't think I wanted to. Taryk may have been my mate, and Celeste my mentor, but Xavier had been my first friend. With the loss of my mother, he was the only true family I had left in any realm.

Yuri reemerged from the tunnel, and we agreed to move back into the castle itself while we were here. Apparently, the room that powered the wards was on another level, and we needed to go up to get to it. We couldn't make any changes to them from here.

Returning to the above ground levels of the castle made my muscles burn and my legs shake like Jell-O. Thankfully my self-healing abilities had begun to come online.

When we reached the level where Xavier had first tried to exit the staircase, he made the left turn. This time, nobody corrected him. He led us through the maze of hallways, following twists and turns that assured I could never make it out of there without a guide. Then we descended again. Luckily, this time we didn't have to go quite so far down.

The spiraling staircase ended abruptly at a large metal door. Xavier worked some magic, and it swung inward. Once we entered, my mouth dropped open. The room was carved out of the solid stone within the ground, not by the work of hands or machines, but nature itself.

Huge crystals and veins of gemstones covered the walls, hung from the ceiling and jutted up from the rock floor. It looked like the inside of a humongous geode. In the center of the room balanced an enormous prism.

"This room powers the wards that protect the castle and the

grounds. Back when my ancestors built this castle, they chose this site because of the discovery of this exact spot. The location had been intended for another building, but when excavation began, and this spot got uncovered, they elected to make this the site of the royal home."

I finally remembered to close my mouth, and my teeth snapped together when I did. Wincing, I continued to stare at the crystals in awe. The prism was completely clear. It looked like its perfect shape had been cut from glass. The rest were all the shades of the rainbow. The colors from the gemstones and crystals bounced off the prism, creating a stunning array of reflections.

Xavier knelt and placed both hands at the point where it met the floor, almost as if he had cupped his hands around it intending to lift it. He murmured briefly in a language I did not understand, and the prism began to twist. As he stepped back, it rotated counterclockwise approximately a quarter of a turn then stopped.

After Xavier spoke another short phrase, runes materialized on the facets of the prism as if they had been burnt in. He stepped back to look them over.

"According to the runes, the wards were set to keep anyone not of the royal bloodline, or not accompanied by such, from accessing the castle or any of the attached grounds..."

He continued to inspect the symbols. "The lands and buildings are in a modified state of stasis... impervious to all manner of magic and assault... hmm..."

I waited impatiently, lamenting the fact that I was unable to read the ancient writing, mostly because I was curious. This was the language of half of my ancestors. I added it to the list of things I wanted to learn some day.

"Okay. The wards were set up to repel any curiosity seekers, but for those who know it is here, which would be pretty much everybody, I would think, it is visible. I am going to change them in a couple of ways. I will leave the main protections the same for safety. Either you or I will have to accompany anyone who wishes to enter. However, I am going to create the illusion of continuity. Everyone who looks in will see the same landscape they have been seeing for all these years."

As he spoke, he used his hands to move and, at some points, erase the runes. He replaced them with new ones, sometimes just changing a part of a symbol.

"On the inside, I am going remove the stasis. The land will again begin to grow and produce food. We will be able to cultivate what we need and support livestock, as well as the creatures we invite inside. I am also adding a shield to keep all magic contained within the boundaries of the wards. To be safe, we will still use as little as possible, but I cannot get this place back on its feet again without some. I am also adding a ward to the tunnel; it will protect our allies and those who mean us no harm, should they need a place to shelter until I bring them inside."

He spent a few more minutes making changes, then stood back and checked it over. He knelt again, and swiping his hand across a slightly elevated stone at the base, revealed a clear cube. He beckoned to me, and I knelt to join him.

Taking my hand, he placed my palm against the upturned

surface. It vibrated briefly, and he let go of my wrist.

“You now have the authority to access and change the wards. It won't do you much good until you learn the runes, but if something should ever happen to me, there are books of them in father's library As they are set up now, you could survive and be safe here indefinitely. My hope is that one day we will be able to lessen them significantly.”

Reversing the sequence he had used to access the prism, he returned it to its original resting place. As we left, he sealed the door then led us up the stairs.

My stomach chose that moment to begin making demands, and I giggled. “So, we can make use of that massive kitchen now, right?”

The others laughed, and Taryk grabbed my hand. “That giant table is as good a place to make plans as any, I suppose.”

Reaching the kitchen, Xavier led us to a massive door. Opening it revealed a pantry the size of the main room at the cabin, full of food that smelled as fresh as if it had been placed there yesterday.

Xavier grinned at my sharp intake of breath. “The stasis applied to everything within the boundaries. This food is just as edible as it was the day we put the wards in place. Help yourselves.”

Nobody needed to tell me twice. Grabbing a basket from a pile near the door, I began loading up. There were fresh fruits and vegetables. Loaves of bread and biscuits. Cured meats, and tiny jars of condiments. My appetite would be appeased.

Once the baskets had been filled, we moved to the massive

dining hall to eat. For a moment I felt a little silly with just the four of us at such a large table.

As the meal wound down, I realized we were coming dangerously close to the time when I would have to say goodbye. Plans had been outlined, and many decisions made. Hopefully the next leg of my journey would be just as successful, and I would return here to find that much progress had been made.

War with the dark mage crept ever closer with each step forward we took. I just prayed we would be ready in time.

Chapter Nine

We stood in the main hall. My leathers had been returned to the version I left the cabin with. My tiara went back in its bag and then into my backpack. I had situated the items from the hidden cache in the dungeon on my person. Our packs had been filled with fresh food since they all knew my appetite well.

Yuri and Taryk were prepared to move on with our journey. Celeste was anxious to see the chateau again. As for me, I was torn. I had an intense desire to see my mother's heritage. To gain that knowledge and perform the invocation that would open my full-strength scribe abilities. But leaving my brother behind broke my heart, even though I knew I would return to him. So far, he had been by my side every crazy step of the way.

We believed our bond would continue to connect us, even across the realms. In fact, we were counting on it. It would be our only means of communication since we did not have a pair of journals available.

I hugged him tightly, refusing to let go even as he attempted to pull away. Speaking through our bond, I tearfully pleaded with him to change his mind and come.

"Please. I don't think I can leave you behind. I need you."

Prying my arms loose, he backed just far enough away to look into my eyes. His voice rang solid in my mind. "You can do this. Taryk is with you. Yuri and Celeste will help you in any way they can. I believe in you. Sometimes being the one everyone is relying on is hard. You do the hard things. Make the hard choices. But it is all for the better in the end. I will be here when you get back."

Only a single tear managed to escape as I nodded. "I love you."

"I love you too. Now go. The sooner you go the sooner you can return."

Turning to Celeste, I opened my mind to the place she wanted me to take us. The room itself appeared to be fairly small. Calling on the ring for help, I brought forth the portal. Celeste popped through ahead of us to be sure it was safe, then beckoned us to follow. Taryk swept me up and carried me through as Yuri zipped ahead of us. I turned one last time to wave at Xavier as the portal winked out of sight.

Turning my attention to my new surroundings, I couldn't help but notice how beautiful it was. And how empty.

"Is anyone here?" My voice came out just above a whisper.

"Most likely not. There are priestesses to serve the reigning scribe when she stays here, but they must be summoned. The magic of the chateau keeps things running smoothly in everyone's absence."

Yuri whistled, and I turned to see what caught her attention. We had arrived in a small alcove that opened into a grand foyer. The sounds of the beautiful fountain that stood front and center reached my ears and had a soothing influence almost immediately.

"This place is a-ma-zing," Yuri pronounced in a whisper not much louder than my own had been. She zipped to the ceiling, taking a look around before returning. "Holy fairy dust. I am impressed."

I grinned at her, and Celeste beckoned us to follow as she started toward the fountain. She reminded me of a tour guide as she introduced us to the areas of the chateau we passed through.

"This is the entry. On the wall opposite are the main doors that we use to receive guests. They lead to the front gardens."

I noticed she used the present tense as if she still welcomed those who had been invited to the residence. She looked thrilled to finally be in her home after so many centuries.

The foyer opened to three hallways, and we took the one straight to the back, opposite the entry doors. "Through here, we have the main hall. Sometimes we threw grand parties here. We had music, buffets of fabulous cuisine, and we danced the night away."

I smiled thinking of my mom at such parties, then grew pensive as I wondered if she'd had the opportunity for such gaiety. So far, I had only heard about the parts of her life where she prepared for the future, and for me. It made me feel better to believe she had indeed had joy in her life.

We continued on, wandering through the chateau as Celeste kept up a running commentary about where we were and what went on in each area. We stopped at a huge bay window to take in the gardens out back. The displays were stunning, and the intricate pathways led to lush green fields lined with white fencing. A gray barn stood in the distance.

"There are horses here?" My excitement ratcheted up a notch or ten.

"Among other things..."

Celeste took a door that opened into a white marble stairwell and led us down. Why were these places always underground?

As if she could read my mind, she answered, "Underground is the most secure option for the things we wish to keep most protected. It is also closest to the universe. Surrounded by the earth, it is easier to draw from its properties and access its gifts."

Thinking of the crystals in the room that controlled the wards at my father's castle, it made sense. It was also the place least vulnerable to any sort of attack. We continued down, Celeste explaining the paintings and tapestries along the way. Taryk and Yuri followed us silently, allowing Celeste and me to share these moments.

When we reached the bottom, an archway led into a beautiful hall. The entire room was done in white. Either side was lined with stunning marble statues.

"Oh!" There were no words for the way they made me feel. "They are beautiful. Who do they represent?"

Celeste reverently touched the only statue to reside in the center of the hall. "They are the Soul Scribes of the past. This is the very first Scribe. Her name was Llewellyn." She pointed out the tiny etched crystal plaque toward the bottom with a name engraved. "Each is created in the exact likeness of the scribe they are meant to personify."

"Where is your statue? I want to see it next." I felt like a little kid asking. I moved down the row, searching for one that looked like her.

She shook her head. "I do not have one."

"What? Why not?" I could not imagine why she wouldn't be included.

"The statue appears in the Hall of Remembrance only when a scribe passes from this world to the next and their soul is released. Because my soul is still bound to this world, I do not have a representation here."

Even though Celeste had made her choice long before I had ever been born, I felt a little guilty. "Will you receive a statue when your soul is no longer bound here?"

"Yes. It is automatic. The soul leaving this plane of existence is what triggers the statue to appear."

While I wanted her to have her statue and be forever remembered in the halls of her people, my heart broke at the thought of her leaving me some day. I didn't know how long she intended to stay with me, but I had been leaning somewhere toward forever.

We walked down the aisle, crisscrossing to pay homage to each statue. As we reached the last statue, I looked up sharply.

“Where is my mother's statue? Why doesn't she have one?” The shrillness of my voice escalated with each syllable I spoke.

Taryk grabbed my arm, and Yuri hovered nervously nearby. I jerked my arm from him and ran back to the beginning of the hall, paying close attention to each nameplate. I recognized a few of the names from the front of the Book of Scribes, and even saw my grandmother's name at the end. But I was too panicked about my mother's statue missing to pay close attention.

“Where. IS. IT! Where? Why doesn't she have one?” I had begun repeating myself as if saying it over and over would make the answer suddenly clear.

“My child, I do not know. We will figure it out. I promise.” Celeste spoke calmly, but the worry on her face belied the tone of her voice. She obviously had concerns over the missing statue as well. Her brows furrowed and lips pursed.

Taryk attempted to pacify me, but I was rapidly losing control. “Everleigh...”

“No. Don't you Everleigh me, Taryk. Do you realize what this means? My mother may not be dead. We have left her this whole time to rot wherever they are holding her! We abandoned her. She needed me and I let her down. What if they are torturing her while I run around the realms like I'm on vacation?”

I knew my behavior needed to be dialed back, but I had stepped off the precipice and it felt like I would fall forever. I could not wrest control back from the hysteria I found myself exhibiting. It wound up being Yuri who saved me from myself.

Once again, I found her directly in my face, and before I could even attempt to swat her out of the way she rubbed her hands together and blew. The brown sparkles were immediately effective. I stopped dead in my tracks, conscious, but it felt like I had been tranquilized.

“I am sorry, Your Highness, but it was for your own good.” I could see on her face that she felt badly about it, but I didn't have the motor skills to respond. Even my brain felt sluggish.

Taryk answered for me as he stood next to me. “Don't be sorry. Thank you. We appreciate that you are willing to do what you felt needed to be done.”

Yuri still flitted nervously about. “Is she going to be angry at me? Will she banish me?”

“No, no.” Celeste tried to soothe her. “She knows you have her best interests at heart. She is simply having a hard time processing this new situation with the loss of her mother.”

I could hear them perfectly and wanted to argue with her that I hadn't lost my mother, I just needed to rescue her. I could get her back. Unfortunately, my lips and tongue were still on hiatus, and I couldn't make a sound. I stood still, desperately afraid for my mother. I whimpered, the only sound I could manage, and Taryk turned to me.

He pulled me against him, saying nothing. He took deep breaths, his cheek resting against the top of my head. He did not say a single word as he waited for my body to respond to his calm. The great hall stood silent. Even Yuri seemed calmed, and Celeste remained placid as always.

Eventually, I matched my deep breaths to his, and my heart rate slowed. The shaking ceased, and I believed myself capable of having rational conversation once more. I tilted my head and looked into his eyes.

"Thank you. I'm so sorry."

"Do not apologize. I know what it is like to lose a parent. We are here for you." His hands slid down my arms to meet mine.

I turned to Yuri. "Thank you. And I am sorry."

She sniffed at me haughtily. "He said not to apologize."

I looked at her with just as much, if not more, attitude. "And I said not to call me *your highness*."

We had a brief staring contest, which we both lost. Smiles broke out at the exact same moment, and I sighed.

"Really, I appreciate your actions. I was losing it, and if I had gone much further, I'm not sure how I would have gotten it back."

She pulled off a classic diva pose and said, "Don't worry, Princess, I'm here for you."

I turned to Celeste. I needed answers. If my mother did not have a statue in the Hall of Remembrance, it meant her soul had been trapped here after her death, or that she wasn't dead and needed rescuing. Either way, I needed to help her.

My stomach felt sick at the thought she might still be enduring pain and suffering while I had been marching forward. Had we come here first, it would have saved valuable time. I said as much, and everyone argued with me.

Celeste shook her head. "You might remember that we exited rather hastily. We went to the place you could make a portal the quickest and safest. It would have made no sense to leave there before doing what needed to be done."

Taryk grabbed my hand and gave it another squeeze. "Ev, we are all doing the best we can, including you. You have made so much progress, and you cannot expect too much of yourself. If she is still alive, she is strong, and we will rescue her. If they captured her soul, we will set it free. I promise."

Tears finally welled up and over. The support I had gotten from everyone still caught me off guard sometimes. Everybody seemed to have this unwavering belief in me. I sniffled. I hated being a crier, and since arriving at the cabin it seemed like I cried all the time. Maybe I could blame all the magic.

"Let's move on then. Let's get this invocation done so we can head out."

Celeste nodded and led us onward. At the end of the hall was an ornate doorway that opened onto another set of stairs. This spiral staircase wound down, and there were paintings of each scribe on the wall as we descended. The portraits stopped well before we hit the bottom, my grandmother's being second to last, and my mother's being the final.

I stopped and stared at it. Her beautiful face gazed out at me. I looked at her and my grandmother side by side and smiled at the resemblance. We all shared the same eyes. I could even see more of my grandmother's features in myself than I did my mother's. Her hair color was similar to mine, and we had the same chin and cheekbones.

“The paintings are unlike the statues. Each scribe's painting appears after her invocation. When we leave the ceremony and head back upstairs, yours will be here as well.”

I grimaced. “Not looking like this, I hope!”

They laughed. Taryk winked at me. “You look stunning, as usual.”

Celeste shook her head. “The paintings appear as the universe wishes. As you saw, none of the others are disheveled or tear-streaked.”

Shrugging, I answered. “Well, there's a first time for everything, and if one were to appear that way, it would probably be me.”

After touching the two portraits reverently, I said my goodbyes and we continued down the stairs. The door at the bottom was made of solid white marble and inset so perfectly into the wall I never would have known it was there had Celeste not put her hand on it. As she made contact, the outline glowed briefly.

“Aperi ianuam.”

At her command, the wall swung open in the shape of an arched door. The room beyond was a world all its own.

Chapter Ten

I thought I had been in awe of the prism and crystals in the castle, but this, this was incredible. The entire room looked to have been carved out of a single crystal. The floor, the walls, and domed ceiling were all spectacular. The circular room was lined with opaque crystal pillars all the way around. On the wall across from the door we entered, a sheet of water cascaded out of the ceiling and disappeared through a cutaway in the floor.

Light emanated from the ceiling as if the room were channeling sunshine from far above. The Soul Scribe crest was etched into the floor in the center of the room. . I made my way over to look at the large crystal podium situated at the top most point of the crest

I silently read the passage carved into the crystal, the one to be read during the invocation ceremony. On either side were depressions for my hands to rest in during the process. From this angle, I could see a white cloak hanging from a spot on the nearest pillar.

Celeste, Taryk, and Yuri had all been standing quietly near the door while I took my time taking everything in. I smiled and beckoned them over.

"Isn't it beautiful?" The words came out in a whisper.

Celeste laughed while the other two nodded. "You don't have to whisper," she teased me. "It's not a library. During the old days, there were often many guests at an invocation, and it could get quite loud in here."

A wistful thought crossed my mind. "I wish I could have seen my mother's. Or my grandmother's."

Shaking off the melancholy, I faced them. We needed to be on our way. While I desperately wanted to spend time in the chateau and learn about my family heritage, I needed to take care of the darkness shadowing every move we made first. Which meant this invocation needed to take place.

"Can we perform the ceremony at any time?" Celeste was my only source of knowledge for how to proceed, and my gratitude for having her with me renewed each time she answered a question, bolstered my confidence, or showed her support.

She shook her head. "No. The rites are always performed by the light of the moon. As the sun sets, the light in the rotunda will wane and be replaced with the soft glow of the moonlight. Only then will the ritual be successful. We have approximately three hours of sunlight left here in

Myntas. I just wanted you to see everything ahead of time in hopes of making you more comfortable. I know you have so much going on right now."

"If you were solid, I'd be hugging you constantly. I cannot thank you enough for everything."

Taryk and Yuri, who had both been silent observers since we entered the room, both spoke at the same time.

"You can always hug me, provided you do not squash me."

"I will hug you any time you need, Ev."

I took both of them up on their offer. How could I not? When you find people who had proven they were on your side, and would literally walk to the ends of the Earth to be with you, you hugged them whenever you could.

"I'd like to take you to a surprise, if you don't have any other way you'd like to spend the next couple of hours?" Celeste led the way out of the rotunda.

"I love surprises."

"Claude ostium." The marble door closed at her command, leaving no trace of its existence in the wall, and we trailed after her up the stairs.

We returned via the Hall of Remembrance, and I made a silent vow to my mother. Wherever she had been detained, we would rescue her. Whether I needed to rescue her body, or release her soul to find its peace, I would do it. That dark mage had made her biggest mistake.

Celeste led us through more beautiful rooms and even hallways that were stunning. Straight to a huge kitchen, whose pantry put even the one at the castle to shame. Taryk and Yuri laughed out loud.

"What?" I asked them indignantly. "Obviously she loves me enough to feed me. That makes her my favorite at this moment."

Celeste joined the laughter. "This is not your surprise, silly girl. I just figured you would be hungry, and it's on our way."

We spent the next twenty or so minutes just relaxing. Celeste told us stories from her time at the chateau and answered our questions. We put aside the impending war and the darkness that had begun shrouding every move we made. It was a welcome respite from the gloom and doom that had been plaguing us.

By the time the meal ended, I felt some of the anxiety had ebbed away. My shoulders were less tense, and the headache that had been threatening disappeared. I could proceed with confidence. We stood, clearing our mess away. It felt like Christmas morning, and I couldn't wait to see what surprise she had in store for me.

With Celeste once again in the lead, we headed toward the rear of the house, where she guided us down another flight of stairs. My forehead wrinkled. I had somewhat hoped for a surprise that didn't reside underground. I felt like I hadn't spent any time in the sun for decades.

We entered a long, plain tunnel, and she gave us a short explanation.

"We believe the dark mage to be hiding somewhere in our realm, so I am reluctant to take you outdoors. This tunnel, however, will get us where we need to go without taking any chances. The chateau is warded against attack, but no point in calling attention to ourselves before we are ready."

It wasn't long before we reached a set of stone stairs marking the end of the tunnel. It appeared to be perfectly sealed as there were no sounds or smells to give me a hint about what she had in store for me.

Resting her hand on the door and speaking the appropriate command caused the door to swing inward and reveal what lay on the other side. We had reached the barn. The tunnel door opened directly into the tack room. The door leading to the main aisle stood wide and I could see the stall doors.

Bouncing on the balls of my feet like a little kid, I did combination shimmy-happy dance in my excitement. All three of the others were gazing at me with amusement.

"What are we waiting for?" I practically pranced down the aisle to the first stall. Yuri kept pace with me while Taryk followed. Celeste was content to stand back and watch.

As I approached the first stall, I sighed in delight as the beautiful head reached out to nuzzle me softly. I stroked her soft neck and ran my hands through her silky mane. Scratching her behind the ears made her whinny and toss her head. As I watched in awe, she spread shimmery wings, reaching from one side of the stall to the other.

"Oh!" I covered my mouth with my hands. "A pegasus..." my

breath seemed caught in my throat. I'd been in love with horses my entire life, but to see a fantasy creature, real and in the flesh... I had no words.

Turning to Celeste, I shrugged as I announced, “And I am crying again. Tears of joy, of course, but tears just the same. I'd hug you if I could.”

After giving one last pat, I moved on to the next stall. I intended to spread the love, and every one of these babies was about to get some quality time with me. Heaven on Earth -or Myntas- didn't get any better than this.

I stopped at every stall. Each had an occupant, and each got some affection. I'd worked my way down one side, and just as I prepared to move to the other row of doors, I got the next part of my surprise.

Unicorns!

I could not believe my eyes. Out of all the chaos and fear, sadness and loss, Celeste had known just what would raise my spirits and bring me joy. I don't know how she knew, but she did. And I would forever be grateful.

Yuri eagerly accompanied me to each door, and none of the animals seemed to be bothered by her presence as she flew to and fro to stand on their backs and run her hands over their smooth coats. Her merry little giggles lifted my spirits even further. Celeste's face shined with her pleasure to see us both so enthralled by the occupants of the stalls.

As a little girl, I had loved the idea of riding on great winged steeds. Horns shining and fur so radiant that it shimmered. I may not have been riding them now, but the potential was there. I'd be crossing that item off my bucket list in the future.

"The barn and fields are protected with every ability we have. The dark mage would love to get her hands on them and drain them of their magic. We believe this herd may be the last in this realm. We will guard them at all cost."

I added these beauties to the lengthy list of reasons she had to be stopped. Now that I knew they existed, I'd be damned if they disappeared.

Only one stall remained, and then it would be time to return to the chateau to prepare for tonight's ceremony. Leaning over the door, I saw a gorgeous gray mare lying peacefully in the straw, her wings relaxed by her side. She raised her head and nickered softly in greeting but did not get up. I talked to her softly, then glanced at Celeste.

"May I go in?"

"I don't know if she will allow it, but you can ask her."

I unlatched the stall door, talking softly to her the whole time. She didn't appear to object, so I entered slowly, and sank to the ground at her head. I stroked her soft fur and scratched behind her ears. As I said I needed to be going, she whinnied and raised her wing.

"A baby!" The precious filly was a soft gray like her mother, with tiny wings. As she lifted her head from its position against her mother, I could see it. She also had a tiny horn growing!

Celeste gasped. "The first alicorn. The time has come." She

looked at me with awe. “One of our few prophesies says that at the time of the birth of the first foal with both a horn and a pair of wings, war is coming. If she survives her first days, we will most likely be victorious.” She left the alternative unsaid. If this baby died, we would fail.

I looked at the tiny foal. She couldn't be very old. Maybe a few hours, a day at the most.

“What should we do? We have to protect her.”

“Come. We must perform your invocation. Once you are the reigning scribe you can command the guard and increase the protections at the chateau. There is no time to waste. The birth of such a rare magical creature will have drawn attention from the dark mage. There is no hiding it.”

Patting her one last time, I made the beautiful new mother a promise. “We will keep your baby safe. I will let nothing happen to her.” I stood to leave, and the tiny baby attempted to stand as well. I waited by the door, and my reward was seeing her take some of her first steps. She toddled over to me on unsteady legs and butted her head gently against my leg. That did it. I was in love. I would die to protect this tiny being.

I knelt, lowering my head to hers and cradling her gently. That contact triggered the bond. Her tiny little tapestry sprang up around us, and we were connected. I could see the love in her thoughts. This tiny being had no fear, no knowledge of the time she had been born into. She reminded me of myself. I would see to it that she lived a long and happy life.

I said goodbye and promised to visit again as I shut the stall door and we headed back to the tunnel. We saw through the skylights that the sun had almost sunk below the horizon and the moon was on the rise. The time had almost arrived.

We returned to the rotunda. As we entered, Taryk asked permission to alter my outfit again, and I agreed. (I hoped to be able to learn this trick for myself in the future.) After all, how many times does a girl get to perform the invocation that will make her the reigning Soul Scribe over all the realms? Once, that's how many. In spite of the circumstances, I intended to try to make it the celebration it should have been.

My black leather became a simple white gown. Yuri fussed with my hair and loosened some curls to fall around my face. Taryk brought me the white cloak from its hook on the pillar, and I was ready. All that remained was to perform the ritual itself.

Nerves set in. My knees felt weak and my handles trembled slightly. The day had come. Long before I had hoped it would, but I would do my best to make my mother and ancestors proud. I reached out along the bond to connect with Xavier.

“Hey, little sister! How are things going on your end? You seem nervous.”

“HA! We are about to do the invocation. Nervous might be a slight understatement. I'm shaking like a leaf.”

“Well—”

“Oh! And there are *unicorns!* And *pegasus!* And the very first alicorn ever born!”

“Wait. What? What’s an alicorn?”

“A unicorn pegasus hybrid. She has wings *and* a horn! We had them in our stories back on Earth, but they are *real* here. I'm in love. She is adorable.”

“A hybrid? There is a prophecy about such a thing... I can't quite recall. I'll have to look it up...”

“Celeste told me of it. Or the scribe version anyway.”

Taryk interrupted our conversation to tell me it was time, and I told Xavier I'd catch him up when we were done here. I looked at the three of them and saw each of them looking back at me.

“You look beautiful. Your mother would be so proud. I'm sorry she is not here to see this day, but I will do my best to stand in for the love and adoration she would be giving you.”

I could actually see the spectral tears running down her cheeks and my eyes welled up. Damn her for tearing my heart out and stomping on it in the best way possible.

Taryk took both my hands in his, after using the pad of his thumb to wipe away the single tear that had escaped my efforts to blink away. He squeezed them lightly and tugged gently, bringing us closer together.

“When I first saw you, I knew you were special. Every moment since then, you have proved there are more layers to you than any onion I have ever encountered. This is just one more step on your path to greatness, and I am honored to be here to witness it.”

The onion reference gave me the giggles, followed by more tears for the sincerity of his faith in me. A tearful smile was the best I could offer him. That and a hug.

Yuri fluttered between us, driving us apart. “My turn. Princess, when I volunteered for this job, I really didn't have much of an idea what I was getting myself into. I still don't for the most part, but seeing how you take each new challenge and meet it head on gives me hope for our future. If the universe has to rely on a single person to save its ass, I'm thankful it happened to be you, and that I get to be a part of it.”

I sniffled. “You guys! Stop making me cry!”

Yuri and Taryk moved off to the side while Celeste motioned me to the podium. “Normally, the person performing the ceremony stands at the pedestal while the inductee stands in the center of the crest. Since you are both, you will stand with your hands in the depressions on either side of the ledge. Simply read the words out loud. The crest will gleam brightly. Do not remove your hands until the lights go dim. That will be it.”

“What will I feel? Does it hurt? When Mom and I first connected the power we exchanged hurt like hell.”

She shook her head. “It feels odd, like your entire being is opened and filled with the new magic, but there is no pain.”

I took my place at the pedestal. Staring at it for a moment. I closed my eyes and sent the thought out to the universe that if my mom could hear me now, let her know I loved her so. I wished more than anything that I didn't have to do this without her, but since I had to, I hoped I didn't let her down.

Placing my hands in the indicated spots, I held tightly and took a deep breath. When my knuckles started to ache, I realized I probably needed to relax my grip some. I read the passage once through in my head before reciting them out loud.

"I am Everleigh, rightful heiress to the power of the Soul Scribe legacy. Oh universe, know my soul, and find me worthy. I accept my reign that begins this night. I am the keeper of balance. The enforcer of the natural laws regarding our magic."

My hands began to feel warm, the temperature increasing as I got further into the passage. My knees, which had already been trembling, threatened to give out and made me grateful for the requirement of keeping my hands on a solid surface. There were only a few more lines. I could make it.

"I am she who will be looked to when magic is endangered. My governance will span all nine realms. There is no territory where I will not have jurisdiction over magic. My place in the universe affords me great power, and also immense responsibility. May I use it only for the good of all creation."

Something began to tell me that there was a whole lot more involved with being a scribe than the book had covered, and I needed a crash course in it, *fast.*

"Ego hoc legatum accipere. Honos habet onus. Animo. Fidem. Ego sum anima scribae!"

The lights in the crest began to appear as I spoke the words in the ancient language. By the time I had finished, the brightness required me to close my eyes. I could feel the magic running through me in currents. With my eyes closed, I could see my tapestry all around me, morphing and changing as the invocation took place.

The magic burned, but not in an overly painful way. It felt almost cleansing as it moved through me. The scribe magic bonded with my fae magic in a way I had never been able to create on my own. Instead of being two strands woven together, they became thicker, stronger, single strands.

The tapestry itself seemed almost an impenetrable bubble when I looked at it. The loose weave had been replaced with a heavier, tighter one. The colors appeared even more vibrant, which I wouldn't have thought possible if I weren't seeing it for myself.

I stood with my hands locked onto the podium and eyes closed until I heard Taryk softly calling my name. It took a conscious effort to relax my grip, and my eyes opened slowly. Oddly enough, once the invocation itself ended, I didn't feel a whole lot different.

“Is that it?” I looked to Celeste for confirmation.

“Congratulations, Everleigh. Let’s return to the grand hall. We must summon the guard and decide what to do to protect our newest arrival.”

I nodded, and the three of us followed her toward the door. Turning back, I took one last look at the room where I had accepted my destiny. My life had just changed drastically, and I was in for one hell of a ride.

Chapter Eleven

Celeste allowed me to say the phrase to close the door, and I felt a little thrill at the feeling that I was coming into my own. As we ascended the stairs, we made a stop. My portrait had, indeed, been added to the wall. But what I saw there shocked me.

I looked very similar to the way I had when the invocation had taken place. There was one glaring difference, however. In the painting, I was wearing a regal crown adorned in jewels of teal and clear crystal. The scribe crest featured prominently in the design. I didn't understand. Scribes were not royalty, as far as I knew.

"Why the crown?" I asked Celeste.

"Perhaps because you are royalty from you father's line. I am not certain, as we have never had a scribe with any other line of magic before. I suppose we shall have to wait and see what the future brings."

"I think it suits you very well," Yuri piped up.

"I agree. You look radiant. Absolutely stunning." Taryk stood staring at the picture with emotion written all over his face. I couldn't readily identify it, but it looked positive to me.

Celeste showed me how to summon the guard, and I stood in the great hall, awaiting their arrival. During the wait, she gave me a summary of how the royal guard worked.

"When they arrive, you will introduce yourself, although it will be just a formality. They will be able to recognize your scribe magic with their own powers. Many of them should know of the prophecy and will understand the seriousness of protecting the little one."

"Jewel. Her name is Jewel."

All three of them looked at me in shock. "It is?"

I nodded. "I was able to learn her name when we bonded. Don't ask me how, I've never been able to communicate with animals before."

Celeste didn't seem surprised. "With your combination of powers, we really shouldn't be surprised when things like this crop up. We will work to refine the skill so we can use it to our advantage. Perhaps you will also be able to speak to other animals as well, now that the power has manifested itself. We shall see. The guard is arriving."

I straightened my shoulders and did my best to appear as comfortable as possible in my new role. I don't know how successful I was, since my insides were in knots and I felt like I might fall over at any moment, but I tried.

A distinguished looking gentleman in a gray suit strode through the door, bowing when he reached me. "How can we be of service?"

I nodded at him. "Thank you for coming. My name is Everleigh. As you have probably guessed, I'm new here."

"You are Amara's daughter? Forgive me, we had no idea her heiress had been born. Where is she?"

His question felt like a sucker punch to the gut, and I was unable to breathe for several seconds. I actually had to bend over and attempt to catch my breath.

Taryk rested his hand on my back and answered for me. "Amara was captured by the forces of the dark mage, and we believe she was killed. She released her powers to Everleigh in her last moments."

The man gasped. "I am so sorry for your loss. She was a great scribe and a great leader. My name is Landon. We will do anything we can to assist you."

Their exchange had given me time to get a grip, and I attempted a small smile. "Thank you. This is Taryk, my magical mate, and Yuri, a trusted advisor. Celeste used to be a scribe and has remained here to assist me as I learn."

While he originally looked surprised that I had a mate, his attention focused elsewhere as Celeste made herself visual and he gasped. "Chosen?"

“I am the Chosen no longer. Everleigh is the Chosen now. The pegasus unicorn hybrid has been born, just hours ago. She waits in the barn with her mother. We must protect her at all costs.”

Landon paled slightly. “The time for war is upon us.”

“Yes, you can see why I called to you. I have bonded with the foal, and we must protect her if we are to be victorious. I will be conferring with my brother, who is at the castle in Amarys, where we are attempting to amass an army to destroy the dark mage.”

“Our forces here will give our lives to protect the filly. The royal guard is made of one hundred men, and one hundred centaurs. There are hundreds of others who can be called up to supplement our soldiers.”

“We will need all the help we can get. I have been informed that we believe the dark mage to be hiding here in this realm. We must be on highest alert. After I speak to my brother, we may attempt to move the foal if we can do so without drawing the wrath of the dark mage elsewhere.” For now, protect her at all costs.”

He bowed and turned to leave.

“Landon?” He turned and waited. “May I ask a favor of you?”

He inclined his head, waiting for my request.

“I am able to bond with others, creating a telepathic link by which we are able to communicate. I'd like to have this opportunity with you. It will allow us to be in contact while I am in the other realms, or even elsewhere in this one.”

He looked at me warily. “You do not make use of journals?”

“I have before, and I will not force you to form the bond. It is simply quicker as you will hear me speak in real time, and absolutely fail safe. It will never fall into the wrong hands, or be misplaced, and no other can hear our communication.”

I saw him hesitate, torn between doing what would be best for his realm, and being wary of becoming forever connected to someone he didn't know. I did my best to put his mind at ease.

“I cannot use this bond to see your thoughts or coerce you into acting in any way. I can occasionally deduce your whereabouts, which is helpful if you are ever lost or captured, but mainly it is for communications. And as I said before, I will not be offended if you decline.”

My explanation worked, and I could see the relief plain on his face. “I would be honored.” He returned to stand next to me, waiting patiently.

I reached out my hand. “It works better for me if we make contact and all you need to do is stand still. There will be no pain.”

I placed my palm on top of his open one and closed my eyes. Calling up his thread came easily, and immediately began wrapping it loosely with one of mine. I wanted just enough to be able to communicate with him.

Once that point had been reached, I called out to him in his mind. He startled, jerking his hand away as he did so, and I deduced that it must have worked. I opened my eyes to see him staring at me in awe.

"I will not intrude on your thoughts unless it is absolutely necessary. I understand how strange it is to have someone else in your head. When I first began to communicate this way, it weirded me out in a serious way."

He laughed a little. "It certainly is strange! I will take our forces to protect the barn. In the meantime, I will let the other troops know to prepare."

"Thank you. Please remember to draw as little attention as possible to your activities, it will be best if we have the element of surprise on our side."

He nodded, bowed slightly at me, then turned to Celeste. "It was an honor to see you." With that, he exited by the same door he had entered.

I turned to her, curious. "How does he know you? He cannot possibly be that old!"

She shook her head. "Oh no. He is not. We live long lives here, but not that long. All of the children in the realm learn scribe history. They have a yearbook of sorts, with our pictures and synopsis of our reign. As Chosen, they learn more about me. It will be the same with you when your time here is through."

That was a strange thought. Children many years from now, learning about *me* in their history classes. The best I could hope for would be that I was victorious in this war, and they would actually have history classes to learn in. If the dark mage won the war, there might not be a future left to study our past at all.

We stood together, discussing the best actions to take next. We needed to get back to the castle and see what progress they had made there, although I was reluctant to leave Jewel here, even with the royal guard watching over.

My stomach growled in protest at the thought of doing anything else before eating. Since the invocation I felt stronger, and hopefully would not tire as easily while performing my magic. But I still needed to eat, and fairly regularly it seemed.

Celeste took us to get food while we talked over plans. I reached out to let Xavier know we would be back soon and got a terse reply. While the brevity of his response was unexpected, he felt busy, not in danger, so I let it ride. He had plenty on his plate as well.

I wanted to return to the barn for a brief visit before we headed back to the castle. I thought it would be a good idea to see if I could bond with Jewel's mother as well. Communicating with an infant would not be nearly as helpful as a conversation with an adult, even if I could get impressions and pictures only.

The others agreed, so we cleaned up our mess and Celeste led us back to the tunnel. On the other side of the door, we saw our first guard. It pleased me to see them taking the matter seriously and guarding the barn from all angles.

When we reached the far end of the tunnel, there was yet another guard, and he announced us, informing us the centaurs had taken up their posts in the barn. My hand tightened on Taryk's arm, more nerves settling in. I had obviously never seen a centaur, and the thought made me anxious.

If I ever returned to live on Earth, I was going to write books about my adventures. Package them up as fiction and they'd probably sell like hotcakes! At least, I would have something to keep me busy for a while.

The thought made me chuckle out loud, which got everybody's attention. “Sorry, guys, my imagination is taking weird turns.”

Entering the barn, we saw at least ten centaurs lining the aisle between the stalls. With their muscular human upper halves and equine bodies, they certainly looked like a force to be reckoned with, and I was glad to have them watching over Jewel.

“Hi, I'm Everleigh. Thank you for coming.”

“Our pleasure, Chosen.” His human half bowed to me.

Approaching the door to Jewel's stall, I murmured softly, asking her mother if I had permission to enter. She whinnied, which I took as affirmation, and I sat down next to her head as before. Jewel settled her tiny body next to me, while I explained to her mother what I hoped to do.

When there didn't seem to be any disagreement, I rested my hand gently on her neck, and reached out with my sight. To my surprise, her threads were very similar to mine. I wondered if she was the pegasus version of the Chosen, seeing as how she had just given birth to the foal that had been foretold in prophecy.

We easily bonded, and I did my best to ensure the connection had more strength than I had formed with Landon. My intuition told me that animals required a more intense bond if I wanted to be able to communicate easily.

Sending my thanks through the bond, I was surprised to hear a voice in a language I could understand. My shock must have been conveyed to her because I heard a giggle.

"*I have lived amongst the scribes most of my life. I learned their language as I grew up. While most of them cannot understand me, I can understand them. And, by the way, my name is Topaz.*"

"This is convenient. Are you aware of the prophecy surrounding Jewel?"

She nodded. "*I am. And I am so very grateful you have provided protection for her.*"

"I am considering taking the two of you back to my brother's castle in Amarys, if that is something you would be open to. The castle is heavily warded, and as far as they are aware, the dark mage has not set foot in their realm for many years."

"*Could we get there safely? Travel is most dangerous these days.*"

"Yes, I would open a portal right from the barn here straight into the castle grounds."

She nodded her head slowly, mulling it over in her mind. "*Anything to make sure my daughter stays safe.*"

We agreed that I would return for her if the castle wound up being the safer place for them. I made sure she knew she could contact me through our bond, even across the realms, and that if they were in trouble I would open the portal straight away and bring them to wherever they would be best protected.

"The second you feel like you might be in trouble reach out to me. I will be here in an instant."

She nodded and I gave Jewel one last snuggle before getting to my feet. Exiting the stall, I let Xavier know we were on our way. He suggested we head to the dining hall since he was having a small meeting there.

I let the guard know I would be opening a portal momentarily, thanked them again. Hopefully there would be no reason for them to engage with the enemy before we got a plan hatched to keep Jewel, and all the other animals at the chateau, safe.

Motioning for Taryk and Yuri to come closer, I opened the portal to my brother's castle. I had learned to make the portal as close to myself as possible, to decrease the amount of distance I had to travel while concentrating on keeping it open. This time I managed to both maintain the portal and take the few steps through it to the other side.

Xavier glanced at me as we appeared not ten feet from him. "Getting stronger all the time, I see."

His comment made me grin. It also made me realize that he spoke the truth. I'd come a long way from the young girl who followed the instructions in a note from a perfect stranger. I still had a long way to go, but I kept proving to myself that I could make it if I believed in myself.

Yuri zipped straight to the table, calling out excitedly. "Uncle Zed!"

They embraced, and immediately my heart swelled to see her reunite with more of her family. It made me so happy to know she still had some here waiting for her.

Xavier sat at the large dining table with a wood sprite, Uncle Zed apparently, a man who looked very similar to himself, and what I could only describe as a gnome. The little man so closely resembled the tiny statues I was accustomed to seeing in the gardens back home that I did a double take.

Xavier stood and made introductions. “As you heard, this is Zed. Queen Flora sent him as her emissary, as she doesn't like to travel far from her tree these days. He was out on patrol the day we made contact.”

He indicated the gentleman on his left. “This is our distant cousin, Solomon. Solomon, meet Everleigh. Ev, I've already told him quite a bit about you. He's staying here for now, so you guys will have a chance to get to know each other better.” I smiled at him and gave a little wave.

“And, last but not least, our representative from the forest gnome colony is Banli. Banli's people are the ones who helped our last dragons go into hiding. He comes as their representative as well.”

Celeste's voice remarked in my head. “The forest gnomes are some of the shyest creatures. They live in homes deep underground within or below the roots of giants trees, and very rarely leave them. I am quite surprised to see one here.”

I nodded his direction. “Welcome. We thank you so much for leaving your home and coming to meet with us.”

He ducked his head, remarking in a sage tone, "Unfortunately, the circumstances demand it. The dark mage must be stopped. If we are to live in peace, we must lend whatever assistance we are able."

His voice turned out to be much deeper than I had anticipated, and his speech was slow and measured. He seemed like the type to not make rash decisions, and I hoped he would convince the dragons to help us.

"We were just wrapping up here. Banli will return to the dragons with our plan, and our plea for their help. Zed has been helping with recruiting, so he will go out and continue doing so. As I mentioned, Solomon is staying here and helping with logistics. I will escort Zed and Banli through the tunnel, and return shortly."

We said our goodbyes, and I expressed my thanks to each once more. Xavier had made good progress, considering I hadn't been away very long. Hopefully we continued to move forward rapidly, and managed to set our plan in motion before drawing the attention of the dark mage.

Chapter Twelve

We were still in the dining hall when Xavier returned from escorting our guests to the edge of the wards. I had planted myself in one of the seats at the giant table, my head propped up in my hand. I couldn't remember the last time I got a full night's sleep, or even a few uninterrupted hours, and in spite of my body's increasing ability to heal itself, I still needed rest.

Xavier took one look at me and told me to take my pick of any of the rooms off the landing upstairs. "They've all been prepped for guests, just in case, so get a few hours of sleep. One of us can always get you if we need to."

A wan smile was my only response as I attempted to stand. It seems sitting down hadn't been my best choice. Maybe I could just sleep right here at the table with my head cushioned on my arms like I used to do when I was a child.

Taryk came to my rescue, tugging me up and sweeping me into his arms. “Let's go, princess. You need some real sleep.”

For once, he wouldn't hear any arguments from me. I just snuggled into his arms, and let my feelings cross through our bond.

“Do you have a preference for which room you're in?”

I simply shook my head, and he nudged open the first door we came to. It had to have belonged to one of Xavier's sisters, done up in shimmering cream and gold. The canopy bed was beautiful, and Taryk eased me down onto the mattress. As I lay back, he removed my boots, setting them beside the bed, and I sighed with pleasure as he rubbed my feet briefly.

The sheets were satiny and softer than I'd ever felt. The mattress was soft as a cloud, yet supportive at the same time. I foresaw some restful sleep in my very near future. Finishing with my feet, he tucked me in, and remained perched on the edge of the bed holding my hand.

“How are you holding up?” he asked me.

I could barely nod as my eyelids were already on their way down. “I'm doing all right. I try not to think too hard about any one thing, and just keep putting one foot in front of the other. I can't wait till we have a chance to relax.”

“When this is all over, I will take you on a vacation. To any realm you want to visit.”

That got my attention, and I peeked out from beneath my sleepy eyelashes. “All of them. I want to see them all. And meet your family.”

His eyebrows rose in surprise. “My family, huh? I think that can be arranged. They're all dying to meet you.”

I opened my mouth to answer, but the only thing that came out was a yawn.

“Sleep,” he whispered. “I'll stay with you until you are out.”

My brain warred with my heart for a moment, but my heart won out. “Stay, please.” I scooted farther onto the bed. “Just lie with me? I don't want to be alone right now.”

He hesitated, if only briefly, and then lay down beside me. Once he seemed comfortable, I turned toward him, settling into his arms. With him, I felt safe. While the stress of recent events didn't leave me entirely, I managed to push them back enough to relax in his embrace.

I tilted my head to look into his eyes. “I am so blessed to have you. Thank you for all the things you have done for me.”

“I'd do anything for you, Ev. Anything.”

Angling his head down, he gently brushed his lips against my forehead, maintaining the contact.

That did it. I was done for. Lifting my chin even higher, I wrapped my arms around him and guided his lips to mine. If I thought the sparks had flown when our bond was formed, this kiss ignited a full-blown inferno.

I felt my magic rise to meet with his. Colors exploded across my range of vision. My entire body was on fire, and I never wanted it to end. His hand tightened in my hair, holding me against him. This may have been my first kiss, but I knew a good one when it stared me in the face.

He pulled back ever so slightly, and I took a shaky breath. "Wow."

We both laughed, and he kissed my forehead again. "Sleep. We can both use the rest."

For the first time since this crazy ride had started, I felt calm and content. Snuggling in close, I closed my eyes and immediately dropped into a deep, deep sleep.

The first clue that something had gone horribly wrong was the smell. Opening my eyes to an almost pitch-black room, the stench of mold and wet dirt stung my nostrils. The air felt cool and damp, which caused me to rub my bare arms in an attempt to be rid of the goose bumps that had risen.

The silence lay heavy, in an unnatural way. Abandoned. Using my sight, I scanned the area for another living soul, finding nothing. The only hint at another possible inhabitant of the place I found myself stemmed from a faint whisper of an aura somewhere farther along the corridor.

Calling an orb of light to my hand, relief filled my chest when it obeyed. I knew I had entered into a dream state again and had no intention of being caught off guard this time. I needed to be as aware of my surroundings as possible without giving myself away. I also wanted to gather as many clues as I could to help us later.

The hallway I found myself in had similarities to the first one, but I knew somehow that they were different, far apart even. I spent a moment trying to get my bearings and deciding which way I should go. I had no idea if I ran into anyone—or anything—if they would be able to see me, or if I would only be a casual observer.

I needed to decide whether I wanted to head toward the possibility of another living being, or away. In the end I decided to creep toward it. Maybe I had been sent here to help someone.

Moving as quietly as possible, which didn't seem very quiet at all in the stark silence, I made my way down the corridor, keeping my light to the absolute minimum. Every few feet, I stopped to be sure there were no sounds other than the ones I had been making.

The passageway led steadily downward. The boldness I had originally been feeling had escaped me, and nerves seeped in. Why had I been put here? What would I find around the bend in the tunnel?

As I reached the turn, I poked my head around just far enough to see. The circular room couldn't have been more than ten feet across, and there was only one other tunnel leading off it. That passage led perpendicular to the one I had come down, exiting off the right side of the room.

The only item in the room appeared to be a table, dead center, about waist high. Approaching it with caution, I turned the light up just a little, shocked by what I was seeing. It looked to be a coffin made of dark crystal resting on an elevated slab of stone.

Shrinking back, my immediate thought was that I had somehow ended up in a crypt. But why? With so little light, I couldn't tell if something rested inside, or if it was empty.

Turning, I had just decided to go back the way I had come when the little voice in my head insisted I stay here. My intuition hadn't steered me wrong yet, but I didn't want to hang out with the coffin for any longer than I had to. Yet it kept drawing me closer. This was what I had been sent to see, whether I understood it or not.

Shuffling closer, I attempted to use my sight. There had definitely been a strong soul inside, but I either didn't yet possess the skill to see what had happened to it, or the dark crystal coffin had the ability to mask whatever it may have been.

For just a moment, I stood there uncertain. Trying to decide the best course of action before I woke and lost the chance to do anything at all stressed me out. Taking a deep breath, I reached out and laid my hand on the crystal box.

Immediately it lit up from the inside, and within a fraction of a second, I heard bloodcurdling screams. I didn't realize they emanated from my own throat until it became raw.

My entire body shook, the spasms creating weakened knees and throwing my balance off. A rush of sound roared through the tiny cavern and blocked out anything else. I closed my eyelids as tightly as I could, praying that I hadn't seen it. That it was a hologram or cruel joke.

As the roaring stopped, I opened my eyes once more. Since I had at some point removed my hand, the crystal tomb on the rock slab had gone dark again. Hesitating, I gathered my courage and reached out once more. Making contact with only the very tip of my finger, I stared in shock as the light shone once more.

There, confined in this prison of crystal, lay my mother. Blood had soaked the side of her shirt exactly where I had felt the stabbing pains during my last vision of her, which was not so long ago. If it had not been for the blood, she would have looked peaceful.

Choking back the tears, I used my sight to see if she still lived. I could not call forth her tapestry, whether because of the properties of her tomb, or some other reason I did not understand. I could, however, detect a faint aura around her.

I began screaming her name, searching all sides of the sarcophagus-like structure for an entry point. Afraid to use my magic to gain entry, lest I set off a trap or harm her, I sank to the floor in frustration.

I began shaking uncontrollably once more.

"EVERLEIGH! Wake! Up!"

Suddenly, I found myself back in the bed in the castle, four sets of eyes hovering over me nervously.

"Stop shaking me!"

Immediately Taryk released my shoulders, and I flopped back into the bed like a dead fish. I stared at the faces around me as I tried to regain some composure. As soon as Yuri asked me what had happened though, I began sobbing again.

"I TOLD you so. I told you. I saw her. They have her..."

Celeste waved the others back a little. "Slow down, child. They have who?"

"My mother. I saw her. The dream transported me into a dirt tunnel. I followed it and found a small circular room with a rock table in the middle." I paused, trying to get enough words in the right order to make a coherent sentence.

Xavier stood at the foot of the bed, watching me closely, while Yuri had flown around to sit on the bed beside me. Taryk still sat at my side.

"The coffin was made of a dark crystal, and at first I couldn't see anything. I didn't know what I should do. I reached out and touched it. As soon as I made contact the thing lit up from the inside and she just lay there."

Another sob ripped through me. The scene had left me feeling as if I had been kicked in the stomach by a mule. Taryk wrapped his arm around my shoulder, pulling me closer. I could feel him trying to calm me, but I just needed to get it out.

"She... She had blood on her. Right where I felt the pain when we saw her in the study. But otherwise she just looked like she was sleeping. She's not dead, because I could see her aura, but I couldn't get to her tapestry for some reason."

Xavier and Yuri both looked concerned. Celeste sat quietly, her brows drawn together in thought.

"I tried to find a latch, or some sort of opening to get her out, but there was nothing. It looked like a solid piece. But there has to be a way in, and out, if they got her in there, right?"

I desperately needed someone to tell me we could get her out and take her home. That saving her from whatever fate they had sentenced her to would be possible.

"Take a deep breath, Everleigh." Celeste attempted to calm me before continuing. "The positive news we have learned is that she is not dead. That means it may still be possible to save her. However, it will not be easy."

"The dark crystal of the coffin sounds like the same material they attempted to imprison the dark mage within." Xavier rubbed his hand against his outer thigh as he talked, a gesture he seemed to do only when his thoughts were occupied fully by something.

Every time I thought I might manage to get the agitation under control, it reared its ugly head in response to one of their comments. This dark mage was going to meet her end, and I struggled with the temptation to run to Myntas and seek her out before we were fully prepared.

"That means the crystal box is not impervious to magic, and there must be a way to release her from it."

"Yes," Taryk mused, "unless she has used her magic to reinforce it. Either way we must try."

"Also," Yuri interjected, "we need to be prepared to heal her. It sounds as if she was injured pretty severely based on what you've told me. They may have put her into stasis when they realized she no longer had the magic they were after, and this is a trap."

Taryk nodded. "I know this will bother you, Everleigh, but are you certain it was her in the box? It's possible that it was an illusion."

"No! Someone was in the box. I could see the aura."

He turned to me fully and grabbed both of my hands in his. "I know. But you didn't see HER tapestry. They could have placed any body into that coffin and placed an illusion spell over it to *look* like your mother."

"But why? How could she know I would come to that place in my dream walking? Until my mom gave me her magic, they didn't even know I existed. And as far as they are concerned, I think my mother is dead."

"The dark mage did not get as powerful as she is by taking chances." Celeste's voice was gentle. "She may have prepared the illusion solely on the off chance that you might happen upon it. We don't know that your touch hasn't sent off some sort of message to her that the place had been disturbed."

"Then we have to go back and get her. Right now!" I attempted to leap out of bed, but Taryk blocked my way.

"Ev, it's not that easy. If she did get notice that the coffin had been tampered with, she could be waiting to ambush us if we go back. We have to be careful."

"Then we have to go right now. Before she has a chance to get anything ready." I started pushing at Taryk, attempting to get him to move so I could get up. "I will just open a portal right into the room and we can bring the whole casket right back here, then worry about getting her out of it and healing her!"

Yuri took the next turn at getting me to pause long enough to think things through. "Everleigh. Stop. You are new at the portal making, so you don't know many of the rules around it. There are some places that can be set to allow you to make a portal of entry, but you will be unable to recreate a portal to escape. One cannot underestimate the dark mage. Please, slow down just enough for us to make sure we have covered all contingencies."

Xavier looked me direct in the eyes, and his message broke through my one-track focus. "Your mother's heart would be broken if you died and lost this war because you were careless. Even for her. She spent her *entire life* preparing for your success. Many people sacrificed, some of them gave everything they had to prepare you to win this. Do not make those efforts worthless."

His words took the air right out of my sails. My shoulders drooped. My butt may as well have been filled with cement, because suddenly, I didn't think I would be able to get off that bed any time soon. He was right, of course.

How could I take the chance of throwing away everything she and so many others had done for me? It was a stark reminder that each and every decision I made had the fate of the world riding on it. Literally. If I screwed this up and the dark mage took over, the residents of all the realms would find themselves sentenced to what amounted to eternal torture.

Before I could verbalize that, his words had gotten through to me, a terrified whinny rang through my head.

"Everleigh, help us!"

"Jewel is in trouble! We have to get back to the stables at the chateau right now!"

Chapter Thirteen

"I am going to open a portal straight into their stall and bring them right back here! Does that work?"

I was already drawing on the ring and preparing to open the portal, before anyone had a chance to answer me. I would not fail them.

Out of nowhere, Xavier produced weapons for himself and Taryk. That reminded me to grab my own weapons from where I had laid them earlier and place them into their sheaths.

"We will need to be prepared to draw the dark mage's wrath, but hopefully she did not appear at the chateau and only her minions will be there. Then she will be less likely to know where they went!"

I sent the mental message that we were on our way, instructing her to bring Jewel and come straight through as soon as it opened.

It took all my focus to make a portal large enough for an animal their size to make it through. The guys stood at the ready with their weapons in case we needed to protect the entrance from marauding forces. Celeste positioned herself at the forefront to guide Jewel and Topaz through, so they would see a familiar face and know it was safe to enter.

Immediately upon opening the portal, we heard the sounds of battle raging on the other side. Celeste ushered the two animals through, and I allowed the portal to snap closed. I sent a message to Landon via our bond that I had removed both Jewel and Topaz from the area and to focus on ridding themselves of the attackers.

"Ask them if they need assistance," Taryk urged.

I did, and Landon declined, letting me know that their reinforcements had arrived, and now that they didn't have to fear for Jewel's safety they would be putting all their efforts into eradicating the entire force that had dared to attack the chateau.

Jewel walked over to me and I knelt on the floor to comfort her. I could feel her fear while they were being attacked and it broke my heart. I snuggled her as I looked up at Topaz.

"I'm so sorry this happened to you."

She snorted. "*This is not your fault, and I cannot thank you enough for coming to our rescue.*"

I looked at Xavier. “Should I open a portal to the great hall where they can walk out to the stables? I haven't been down there yet, so I can't make one directly to it.”

“How about directly into the garden?”

I nodded then looked at Topaz. “There is no more highly protected place to be in any of the realms. You will be safe here, and if any problem should arise, I will be here to zip you right out.”

Giving Jewel one last hug, I stood, and prepared to open the portal. The ring’s familiar power rolled through me, and in seconds we were looking straight through the bedroom wall into the open gardens. Topaz nudged Jewel to encourage her through. Exhaustion got the better of me, and I lost my hold on the portal before I was able to follow them through.

Sighing, I shrugged. “Looks like it will be the stairs for me.”

Taryk laughed. “The rest of us too, apparently.” I elbowed him gently, and he grabbed my arm.

As a group, we headed out to make our way to the gardens. Stomach grumbling, I veered toward the kitchen to make a pit stop as we reached the bottom of the stairs. Xavier, Celeste, and Yuri smiled. Having already eaten while I was dreaming, they agreed to meet us in the gardens.

Grabbing a basket off the counter, I proceeded to the pantry with Taryk close at my heels. As soon as we were shielded from sight, he grabbed me by both shoulders and looked me right in the eyes.

“Are you really okay? I worry so much when you go into those dreams. That's the one place I can't protect you.”

My heart nearly burst. Tears welled up in my eyes. This man was making it impossible not to fall for him. I tried reminding myself that I needed to avoid distractions, but it didn't appear to be working as well as I had hoped.

I could barely make words, so I nodded. He pulled me closer and wrapped me in a hug.

I hadn't realized how starved I'd been for physical affection since my adoptive parents had passed away. The hugs and gentle touches I'd been receiving since making my way to the cabin were filling a void I had barely acknowledged existed.

Add the romantic gestures since Taryk and I had been spending more time together and my heart warred between being full of love for the ones around me, and full of grief for the losses I had already suffered. My brain told me not to get too close to anyone, because a war of this magnitude would most definitely cost us some lives, and I didn't know if I could handle losing anyone else right now.

A single tear managed to escape, and he wiped it away gently with his thumb. I'd left the bond open, allowing him to feel the struggle within me. He raised my chin, then pressed his lips to mine. Eyes wide open, this was not a kiss of passion, but of promise.

Separating, we grabbed snacks to go. I'd already spent plenty of time in the pantry and I wanted to get Jewel and Topaz settled into their new home, so we could plan more of our strategy; I wanted nothing more than to end this dark mage's reign of terror once and for all. I needed to check in with Landon again as well.

Entering the garden, we saw them standing there, Jewel playing in the green grass. She looked as if she had not a care in the world, as it should be for babies. Stopping, I stood and admired her for a minute. Once we began moving again, I made sure to reach out through our bond so as not to startle her when we approached.

Our group proceeded down the path to the stables. Once inside, Xavier directed us to the best stall for the pair.

“It's got plenty of room, and your own access to the paddock outside.”

Both Jewel and her mom looked ready to settle down for a nap after the upheaval of earlier. Making sure they had all the things they could possibly need to be comfortable, I gave them some final affectionate pats, and we headed out the door.

“Anything you need, anything at all, just call me through our bond. I will not leave the castle grounds without first letting you know. You will be safe here.”

We heard no other sound but the crunching of our feet on the gravel path as we returned to the castle en masse. I didn't know the others’ thoughts, but I mentally made a to-do list as we walked. Getting my mother back to the castle, whether in that crystal coffin or out, made the top spot on the list. I wouldn't be able to concentrate on anything else until I knew she rested safely away from wherever they kept her.

Landon contacted me before I made an attempt to connect with him. “All is well here, Chosen. The forces who survived were driven back to wherever they came from, with the exception of one, who we reserved for questioning. Would you, or your representative, wish to be present for the questioning?”

“Thank you, Landon. Yes, one of us should be. Give me a moment to confer with the others and I will let you know.”

As we entered the castle, I turned to the others. “Landon, the head of the guard at the chateau, has a prisoner from the attack. They will wait to question him until one of us can be present. Who should go?”

There were looks all around the table. I decided to begin. “Obviously I need to go for transportation purposes, unless someone has a travel method other than a portal?”

Everybody nodded. Celeste spoke up. “I will obviously go with you. And we need one of the men. Yuri can stay or attend as she pleases.”

“I believe I will stay, if Xavier will escort me through the ward, I would like to have a meeting with my grandmother.”

“I guess that leaves me as your travel buddy,” Taryk said with a wink.

I sent the message to Landon letting him know we would arrive shortly.

Yuri flitted nervously. “Be careful. She is a sneaky being. Never let your guard down, even in the chateau. I plan to ask my grandmother what she remembers of the imprisonment of the dark mage. Hopefully she will have some helpful information for us regarding your mother's situation."

"Thank you, Yuri. I cannot tell you how much I appreciate you. You be extra safe as well. We never know when she is going to turn her attention this way."

Xavier gave me a hug. "Running off again, are you? Can't seem to keep you in one place now that you have that blasted ring." We laughed together. "Seriously though. Be careful. If you need me send word though our bond and open the portal. I will be by your side in an instant."

"I know, and I will be. Keep your eyes peeled as well. We are doing more and more that has the potential to draw her attention to us, and no matter how well protected we are here, she has the knack for making trouble. Keep Jewel safe, no matter the cost."

I took a deep breath, gathering the power of the ring. Creating portals so close together was drawing on my reserves, and I would still need to be able to make our way back in a fairly short time. Yuri, ever my rescuer, flew up and handed me a tiny bag.

"Keep this in your pocket in case you need a little pick me up while you are gone." She winked at me and returned to Xavier's side as he headed toward the tunnel.

"Thank you!" I called to her and slipped it into my jacket.

Taryk and I linked hands, and I opened the portal into the great room of the chateau. I announced our arrival via the bond, and Landon appeared momentarily from a hallway we had not used during our first visit.

He nodded at Taryk and then bowed toward me. “Thank you for returning, Chosen. This way, please.”

We followed him the way he had come, entering a steep stairwell that led below the chateau. I had a brief moment of panic, wondering if we were entering a torture chamber similar to that at the castle. Taryk felt my pause, and squeezed my hand, letting me know to relax, that he would take care of it if that happened to be the case.

We had barely finished the exchange when we arrived at a solid door. I let out the breath I hadn't realized I'd been holding when it was a bare room on the other side. The prisoner sat in a large metal chair, chained at the hands, feet, and chest.

“He is magically restrained as well and shielded from being able to make contact with anyone outside this room.” Landon strode up and stood directly in front of the chair. The prisoner kept his eyes trained on the ground.

While he studied the floor, I took the opportunity to study him. He was humanoid, although far larger than any man I had ever seen. He wore no shirt, just pants and combat type boots. His hands were proportionately larger than a human as well.

Landon stood before him, arms clasped in front of him. “We can do this the easy way or the hard way. The choice is yours. But you will make it now. I don't have the patience for your games. Who sent you?”

Via our bond, I heard him tell me that he intended to start easy with a question or two, but then it would get serious very fast. If I wanted to leave the room, he understood. I relayed the message to Taryk, who announced he would stay even if I had to go. He had some tricks of his own to help get the information we needed.

My stomach turned inside out at the thought, but I knew I needed to see this through. We needed every edge possible, and this captive presented a big one. I nodded at him to continue.

Silence from the chair.

“Last chance. This is about to get very unpleasant for you.”

I was startled to hear a gruff voice from the chair. “Not nearly as unpleasant as if she knew I was talking to you.”

Landon inclined his head. “So the dark mage *did* send you?”

Realizing his mistake, the creature in the chair scowled, pressing his lips together.

Landon asked a few more questions, but there was not another peep from the guy in the chair. Apparently she was way scarier that he could ever be. So, Taryk took a chance and stepped forward. Landon stepped back in return.

He began pacing in front of the chair, adopting a conversational tone. “Depending on how long you've been around, you may have heard about the first time the dark mage was imprisoned.”

That statement caused an immediate stiffening of the man’s (for lack of a better term at the moment) body. He raised his eyes and stared at Taryk suspiciously.

“The tales of the great mage who captured her have made their way around the realms ever since.” Taryk turned to face the chair, drawing to his full height, and seeming even taller than I had ever remembered him being.

“That mage was my father. When he passed from this world, I inherited his powers, plus the ones I bear from my mother's line.” At this point the captive was visibly attempting to wrest himself from the bonds that held him. All I could do was watch in awe. I had never seen this side of him, and I had to admit I felt both pride and a little apprehension.

Taryk began to give off a glow, minute at first, but growing brighter every second. “You do not want to incur my wrath.” His voice boomed, echoing off the bare walls of the chamber.

Even Landon startled visibly at the sound, looking at Taryk's back with surprise on his face. I then watched him as he nodded, seemingly in agreement with the tactics being employed. Taryk extended his hand toward the prisoner. There was nothing visible happening, but the big guy started shaking his head, eyes shut tightly.

“Do you wish to answer our questions, or do you need more persuasion?”

Taryk paused for a moment, but there was no other sound or movement from the chair, save the frantic shaking of his head.

“Last chance...”

“OKAY!” The word burst forth, almost as if it came against his own will. “But you must promise to kill me when you are done. Do not let her get her hands on me again.”

Taryk's theatrics lessened, until he once again appeared to be the man I had always known. He looked over his shoulder and motioned Landon forward.

“Where is she hiding?” Landon dove straight into the important questions, most likely hoping to get answers before the fear faded.

“I don't know,” the gruff voice replied sullenly.

Taryk took a step forward again, reaching toward the prisoner.

“I swear I don't!” The gruff voice had an amazing range, for this response was even higher pitched than I would have managed. “Very few know, and I am but a lowly pawn in her game. It is said that she never ventures from her lair and has only one or two trusted advisors there. They take turns going out to meet with the higher ups who pass the messages along to us peons.”

His voice rang bitterly, and I almost felt a moment of pity for the poor creature. I could not imagine how terrible it must be to be trapped under her thumb.

“The rumor is that she does not feel she is yet strong enough to wage war and be successful. She attempted to capture the Soul Scribe magic but failed. The magic was passed to a successor the mage did not know even existed. Her fury was felt by all that day.”

I nearly jumped out of my skin when he mentioned the attack on my mother. I wanted to march up to him and choke the information out of him, but Taryk's soothing presence in my mind kept me where I stood. These two knew better than I how to extract information.

Now that he had begun to speak, the words couldn't come fast enough. “There is a rumor that the next scribe will be more powerful than any creature the realms have ever seen. It is said that she will receive magic not only as a Chosen Scribe but from a mighty king as well. The dark mage wishes to see her dead before she is able to come into her powers.”

Landon interrupted him. “Why were you sent here to the chateau?”

“Nobody has been able to locate or identify this scribe. The dark one heard that a prophecy regarding the birth of a hybrid, resulting from the mating of a pegasus and a unicorn, had been fulfilled. She believes that if the foal is killed, she will be victorious in her quest. Our job was to capture it if possible so the dark one could absorb her magic, or kill it if we had no other choice.”

His head hung then, dropping to his chest rather suddenly. For a moment, I thought he had perished in front of me. Then he lifted his eyes, meeting mine directly.

“Please. Kill me now. I have told you all I know.”

I shook my head slowly, a thought forming in my brain. I requested via the bond for the three of us to step outside for a moment, if someone else could stand guard briefly. Landon summoned a replacement and we stepped into the hall.

“I had originally thought to attempt to create a one-sided bond with him and return him to her,” I began.

“No.” Taryk's interjection was firm. “It is too risky. The last thing we need is her to get her hands on a creature who is bonded to you. She could—"

I held up my hand. "If you would let me finish?" He nodded, looking slightly guilty. "Thank you."

Looking at Landon, I continued. "I assume she has some sort of control over the forces she sent here?"

He nodded. "We believe the only reason he still lives is because we brought him directly to the shielded room. We managed to capture two before him, and they both dropped dead within minutes of us laying hands on them. This one had been injured and could not escape fast enough. We brought him directly here knowing this room would null any spell she had put on him. As you can see, he has survived thus far."

"The wards over the entire castle would have the same effect as this room does, right?" I looked at Taryk.

He nodded thoughtfully. "I think so. We'd want to double check with Xavier to be sure."

"Why don't we return him to the castle and put him in the dungeon downstairs? We can alter the cells slightly, so they are less barbaric, and he can stay there until the war is over. I hate to have to kill him, and I know we cannot turn him loose, even though he doesn't know who I am yet."

Landon looked shocked at my suggestion. "Chosen, I dislike arguing with you, but this is not like finding a stray puppy that you wish to give a home."

I giggled at the image. “Do not feel like you can't speak your mind with me, Landon. I appreciate those who are willing to tell it like it is. I may be making it obvious that I am not cut out for war, but I couldn't live with myself if we killed him for no reason.”

“No reason?” Taryk's incredulous voice broke in once more. “He attempted to kidnap and kill Jewel. Remember her, cute fuzzy little thing with a pair of wings *and* a unicorn horn?”

I frowned his way. “Why no, my memory must be faulty...” He had the good grace to look slightly chagrined but did not apologize or change his stance.

“Landon is right. This is not a stray puppy. Redcaps are very dangerous creatures.”

“Redcaps?”

Landon spoke up. “Redcaps are a breed of gnome. The dark mage magically changed them as part of growing her army. They are much taller and meaner than normal.”

“I am going to ask Xavier what he thinks.”

Turning my conversation inward, I reached out along the bond with my brother to get his opinion. After a brief back and forth with him, my decision was made.

I looked at the two men. “Xavier is reinforcing the dungeon wards and spells as we speak. He says we can always kill him later if the need arises.” The last half of my sentence almost choked me, but I knew it would go a long way to convincing Taryk.

Both guys shrugged their shoulders, neither looking entirely convinced, but not arguing either.

"So be it."

Chapter Fourteen

"How will you get him back to the castle?" Landon asked.

"A portal, I suppose. The same way we planned to get back. He'll need to go straight from one protected space to another, and I will make it directly into the dungeon on our end."

Landon looked thoughtful. "You cannot make a portal into or out of this room. The protections will not allow it. And I have a feeling if he sets foot outside the door, he will drop dead."

Details, details. Pesky little buggers.

"And," Taryk added, "how will we be sure he cooperates? We can't just drag the whole chair there."

Celeste, who had not shown herself, nor made a peep during the entire trip here, manifested beside me and spoke up. “Perhaps, my child, you should give him a choice.”

Landon visibly startled at her appearance, which made me smile. “A choice. Prisoners don't usually get choices.”

She nodded at him. “True. But Everleigh has yet to strip magic from a soul. When it comes to cooperation, if she were to take his magic from him, he would be less of a threat to move to the castle. She needs the experience, and this would be a good one. He can have his magic stripped and move to the dungeon, or choose to pass from this world.”

“If Ev needs the experience,” Taryk suggested, “perhaps she should strip the magic either way.”

My heart constricted a little at the thought of stealing a creature’s magic, even a prisoner. Even one who could cause me great grief if I left him with it. Even one who was going to die anyway. I really did not seem to be cut out for war. I couldn't argue with his logic though. I needed to begin mastering all the skills I possessed in order to become capable of beating the dark mage.

“And,” she continued, “she should be able to create a portal in the room. Her Chosen magic should override any other here at the chateau. There is nothing she cannot do here within these wards.”

I looked at her. “Will that be true even though my ability to make portals comes from my Fae magic?”

“It should be. Once the invocation was performed all your magic became one. There is no longer a distinction between one half of your magic and the other. There is only you, as Chosen, and your magic.”

"I'm sorry to rush you," Taryk began, "but we do need to get moving. There are pressing matters to be dealt with back at the castle."

Taking a deep breath, I turned toward the door. "Let's do it then."

We strode back into the room as a collective and stopped before the chair. The prisoner looked up. "Are you going to kill me now?"

I stepped forward. "You have a choice. I will strip you of your magic, and you can return to our dungeon for the duration of this war. When the dark mage is defeated, you will be free to return to your lands. Or you can choose death, right now."

He looked at me, shock clear on his features. His mouth opened, but no words made their way out. It made me wonder what his existence had been like up to this point.

After a brief moment of working his mouth like a fish out of water, he finally managed to form a sentence. "I would rather die than go back to your dungeon to be tortured."

I shook my head. "No. No torture. Confinement, yes. But I will make your cell comfortable, and you will be fed and treated fairly as long as you do not try to cause problems for us. I can't take the risk of setting you free now, but once her reign of terror has ended, you may return to your life, and your family if you have one. I will even return your magic to you."

His suspicion was obvious. He sat staring at me in disbelief, brows drawn together and lips pursed. "There is no way to return magic to a person once it has been stolen. You are a liar."

I took a step closer and leaned in close, whispering. “That is true... for everyone but the reigning Chosen Soul Scribe.” Once the sentence had been uttered, I returned to full height, arms crossed and waiting.

Eyes wide, he nodded after a brief hesitation. “I will go to your dungeon. You should know there are many who wish to escape her clutches. You may find allies in the most unlikely places if you are looking for them.”

Glancing at Taryk and Celeste, I just nodded at his statement. I was too busy praying that I would be able to successfully strip his magic without hurting him since I had never attempted to use this particular skill before.

Celeste could feel my worry and did her best to give me comfort via the bond. Her instructions were clear, I just hoped I followed them correctly.

I positioned myself near the chair, explaining the process as I did so. “This won't hurt. I am going to lay my hand on your shoulder-”

Landon interrupted. “I'm sorry to interrupt, Chosen, but you should not touch him before his magic is stripped. The dark mage may be able to access you in some way with physical contact.”

Acknowledging him with a tilt of my head, I continued. “I will simply pull forth your magic, separating it from you. I will then hold it until such time that I can return it to you.”

Without waiting for an answer, I closed my eyes and pulled his soul into view, hoping to find what I needed quickly and easily. The colors were muddled and ran together like an ink drawing soaked by the rain. I could see the dark strands shot through the weave, indicating how much influence the dark mage had exerted.

After conferring briefly with Celeste, we decided to remove the magic and leave the dark mage's other work. Removing it could alert her, and once he had no magic, she would have nothing to control. Since he would be in a shielded area for the remainder of the time she would be a threat, we weren't worried. I knew I could always go in and remove those strands later if we deemed it necessary.

Pulling the magic out proved to be easier than I expected, and it took only a minute. Opening my eyes, I informed him that I had finished.

While I didn't feel as worn out after doing that much magic as I would have previously, I still felt the drain. I excused myself to step out into the hallway for a moment, thankful Yuri had sent me with a little pick me up. I pulled the tiny pouch out of my pocket. Briefly, I felt like I had hidden myself to take illicit drugs, but laughed it off.

Feeling better, I returned to the room and prepared to create the portal home. Before doing so, I let Xavier know we would arrive shortly, and he agreed to meet us downstairs.

“I have altered the wards and added some specifics to the dungeon area. I also reformed the cells as you asked.”

“Thank you. See you in a minute.”

Taryk addressed our prisoner briefly. “We are going to remove you from the chair and bind you magically. You are expected to behave as docile as a newborn lamb, or I will snuff out your life where you stand. Are we clear?"

The redcap simply nodded.

I rested my hand on Taryk's arm, pausing him briefly. "Do you have a name?" I asked the prisoner.

Again, his surprise was evident on his face. "Angus."

"Okay, Angus, let's proceed."

The process went off without a hitch, and Angus did exactly as he was told. After saying our goodbyes to Landon, I opened the portal directly to the dungeon hall, and we stepped through. Xavier and Solomon waited for us.

Solomon immediately reached out and grabbed Angus's arm, yanking him roughly and pushing him against the wall.

"HEY!" I stepped between them and blocked Solomon as Taryk took his arm and moved him back.

"What?" He snarled at me and yanked his arm out of Taryk's grasp.

I looked toward Xavier with raised brows. What the hell was this crap? Taryk had positioned himself between Solomon and me and watched him with a wary eye. I could see him struggling not to sock the Fae in the face for touching me. But he let me handle it, and that impressed me greatly.

"I will *not* put up with this treatment of *anyone* within our care. Do I make myself clear?" I stood my ground, and there was no way anyone would be challenging me on this. Not if they knew what was good for them.

He gave a sarcastic laugh. “I'd like to know why you think you're the boss around here.”

Xavier chose that moment to step in. “Because she is the Royal Princess of this realm, and you will treat her as such! Apologize, NOW!” The power he pushed forth was impressive, and I loved knowing he had my back.

Solomon shot him an exasperated glance. “Fine. Sorry.” It sounded insincere at best, but I elected not to push it.

“Which room are we putting Angus in?”

“Room? This isn't a hotel, *princess.* They are cells.” Solomon's attitude grated on my nerves.

I hadn't had any restful sleep in ages, my stomach demanded to be fed again, soon, and my emotions were running high after seeing my mom in the dream world. The temptation to sock him in the nose myself had become almost impossible to ignore.

Xavier saved the day. With an exasperated sigh, he instructed Solomon to head upstairs and wait for him in the library. With a last dirty look in my direction, which garnered a glare from Taryk, Solomon stalked back down the hall and through the door to the stairs. I had no doubt in my mind that if he had been able to slam the door like a petulant child he would have.

Xavier led us to one of the middle doors. “Here we are. I

enlarged it and made it as comfortable as possible."

I had to admit, the result left me impressed. Gone was the damp feeling in the air, and the musty smell had abated as well. The room held and actual bed, plus a chair and small table.

Turning to Angus, I smiled. "I know it is still a cell, but we really are trying. Are you hungry?"

The over-sized goblin stared at me as if he waited for me to tell him I had been joking and intended to kill him after all. It took him a moment, but he did respond. "Your Highness, thank you. I am hungry."

His gruff voice covered what I would have bet to be real emotion, not that he would ever admit it out loud. I felt good about having done right by him no matter what manner of creature he was.

"A meal will be sent down momentarily."

He settled himself in after his magical bindings were removed. As Taryk swung the solid door shut, I caught him stretching out on the bed.

The three of us moved down the hallway and stood at the bottom of the stairs. We needed to have a meeting amongst ourselves before heading back to deal with the issues upstairs.

"So. Wanna tell me what our so-called *cousin's* problem with me is?" I let my full irritation show.

Xavier shrugged. "I'm not totally sure, but it probably stems from the fact that as one of the few living descendants of our father, he had hopes to take over the throne when the dark mage was finally defeated. Now not only do I stand in front of him, so do you."

"Do you really think it's wise to have him involved in any of this then? How do we know we can trust him? You may know him so he might feel some loyalty toward you, but he probably wouldn't hesitate to accidentally help me disappear." I had genuine concerns over his trustworthiness, relative or not.

"Because he knows that I will kill him on the spot if he jeopardizes your life or safety in any way. No questions asked."

While I felt a little better knowing Xavier had my back, it still wouldn't make me any less dead if Solomon had nefarious plans. I made a mental note to always be on guard, just to be on the safe side.

Taryk's voice rang out through our bond as well. "I won't ever leave your side. And I will put the fear of my wrath into him next time he dares be disrespectful to you." Giving them both a grateful smile, we headed up the stairs to put out whatever fires awaited us.

Yuri announced her return as we started, so Xavier left to meet her in the tunnel. As Taryk and I climbed the stairs, I expressed my concern over Solomon. Not just for my own safety, but that of Angus, and whatever other creatures may find their way to our dungeon. He was untrustworthy at best, and downright dangerous, at worst.

Without being asked, Taryk steered us for the kitchen upon exiting the stairwell. He instructed me to sit down in one of the chairs and proceeded to make me a plate of all my favorite things and brought it to me.

Through the big picture windows, I could see all the way to the stables and watched as Jewel made her way out into the paddock. She leapt and pranced as if she were a kitten, and I laughed out loud at the sheer joy of it. Even from this distance I could see she had grown, and it made me wonder just how long we had to keep her alive for the prophecy to be fulfilled.

I wanted her to be around forever, but it would be nice to check one major thing off the list. I didn't even know how long unicorns, or pegasus, lived.

"Do you know?"

Taryk shook his head. "Not exactly. Both unicorns and pegasus can live a couple hundred years, but as with any hybrid or new species it is hard to say which rules will apply to them, and which rules they will write for themselves. Just like you."

"I need to get more practicing in. I've been running around doing all these things, which has been necessary, but there is still so much I cannot do. Or do well. We need every advantage."

"I will be with you, but you're right. I want to be sure you can defend yourself at the very least if we somehow get separated."

Before we could go any further, Yuri came zipping out of the stairwell. "Hello! I missed you. How did it go?"

Filling her in briefly, she about crash landed when Taryk informed her our newest resident was a magically altered redcap goblin.

"What?" That sprite had the ability to shriek at decibels that would probably make most human eardrums bleed, and mine protested every time.

Once the ringing had ceased, I answered her calmly. “I stripped him of his magic, and he will live in the dungeon until the dark mage has been disposed of. After that, I will free him to return to whatever life he wishes to live.”

Xavier exited the staircase a moment later, followed by Banli, effectively cutting off any argument Yuri may have been preparing. Surprised to see him, I stood in greeting.

“Your Highness, I have come from a conference with the dragons.”

Xavier pulled up a couple more chairs, and invited Banli to sit. I tried not to show just how nervous I had become at the very mention of the awesome creatures.

Once we were seated, he began to relay the message.

“The dragons are not opposed to assisting with the war against the dark mage. However, before they will commit, they have one request, and it is non-negotiable.”

My stomach took a nose dive. My only knowledge of dragons came from the fairy tales we had on Earth, and none with a request.

Banli turned to me. “They request an audience with you.”

“What?” My high-pitched squeak probably rivaled Yuri's. Oh no, no, no. Nope.

My panicked inner dialogue was gently interrupted by Taryk's smooth voice in my head. His advice? Just listen to the gnome, and then we could work out what to do. No need to panic before we knew exactly what they required of us.

Xavier responded, calm and collected as always. “They are always welcome here at the castle. Any time they wish to come, we would welcome them.”

I shot him a grateful glance. Thank goodness I would have everybody else with me.

Then Banli continued. “They have no desire to leave the safety of their hiding place. They wish for her to come to their lair. Alone. As soon as possible. They believe that time is short.”

Taryk spoke first. “I'm sorry, but that is impossible.” His vice was flat and left no room for argument. “Everleigh cannot leave the protected grounds of the castle. It would put her at risk for attack and possible capture. If that were to happen, the war would be over before it even began. It could plunge the realms into centuries of darkness.”

Banli held up his hand. “We are willing to allow the Chosen to create a portal directly into our hidden home. From there, we will lead her to the dragons. The dragon wards extend to our lands. She would simply move from one warded place to the next.”

Taryk spoke in my head as I pretended to ponder the situation. “This is unprecedented. Their homes are so strongly warded, none could ever break them. Portals into or out of them are strictly forbidden for their safety and seclusion.”

“I'm sorry, but there is a problem. I can only create a portal to a place I have seen before. The only time I have been able to create one to a new place was by viewing the place we were going through the shared memories of someone I am bonded to.

“Perhaps you and Banli could create a bond?” Xavier suggested.

He shook his head. “I am sorry, Chosen, please do not take offense, but such things are against our very nature.”

“None taken.” We seemed to be at a stalemate. There was no way I could make a portal to a place I had never been.

“Perhaps I can be of service?” Yuri raised her hand and waited for all of us to look at her before continuing. “The princess and I are already bonded. If it would not be against the gnomes wishes, I am willing to be taken to the edge of their lands, blindfolded, or subdued as necessary. I can then project the image to the princess. Once she opens the portal, she and I can trade places, and I will return to the castle before she allows it to close. She will have no trouble creating a portal home when she is finished.”

Xavier and Banli both nodded slowly, seemingly mulling over the idea. Yuri had a good point. I would be able to create the portal that way. But I was scared to death to be alone outside the castle wards. And even more scared of being eaten or toasted like a marshmallow. But we needed the dragons’ help more than any other creature. If we did not get their assistance, we could not be victorious.

Taryk shook his head in the negative while Banli and Xavier both voiced their agreement.

"I will go with her. She cannot leave the wards unprotected." Taryk had drawn himself up to his full height and did not look like he would be backing down.

I put my hand on his arm. "It's okay. I will be okay. Everything will be okay. It will work out and then everything will be okay-er than okay."

I looked into his eyes, and used the bond to be sure he knew every last thing I felt at that moment. It had to be done, whether I liked it or not. I had to show that I believed myself worthy of their trust and their commitment. If I couldn't even bring myself to meet with them, how on Earth would I be able to face down the dark mage and come out on top?

It was time to put on my big girl panties and get ready to face my fears.

Chapter Fifteen

I pulled Yuri aside to thank her. What she offered to do had made a difficult task that much easier. As we said our goodbyes, Banli approached me. It would take them only a couple of hours to reach the borders of his land, and he requested I bring no weapons with me. I paused, wondering about the dagger guaranteed to kill the dark mage, but figured I would bring the potion and the pendant, which would at least ensure I made it through to battle another day.

"Thank you. We sincerely appreciate that you are willing to be of assistance."

He simply nodded and turned to follow Xavier and Yuri to the stairwell. Yuri waved, smiling. At least she didn't seem overly concerned about her situation. I, on the other hand, teetered on the edge of a nervous breakdown.

Taryk and I moved to one of the sofas while we waited for Xavier to return. He held my hand tightly, his worry strumming through our bond. I could almost feel the vibrations of his emotions.

"If anything happens to you, I will never forgive myself."

"I am going to be fine. The plan is close to foolproof, as long as I don't anger one of them and cause them to swallow me whole." Cue the nervous laughter.

"They will not roast you alive. But I cannot help the concern over sending you out there with no protection. Neither the gnomes nor the dragons have made an oath to protect you should the need arise."

"True. But I have my intuition. Every time I have been even slightly in need of defense, my self-preservation instincts have kicked in, and some degree of magic has saved my butt. I will be wearing the pendant to protect me from any of the dark mage's powers and carrying the potion. I remember my shielding, and my offenses are getting stronger each time we have practiced. If all that fails, the portal to home is a step away."

"Remember you cannot make a portal within the dragons' lair, so you will have to make your way out of there first. But getting home should be your first objective, not fighting."

"Cannot, or should not? I may be able to create one there, bad manners or no. I will attempt a portal home as soon as I feel I am in danger, wherever I am. I promise."

He leaned in close, resting his forehead against mine. "I cannot live without you. Please be careful."

“I promise.” Brushing my lips softly against his, I let him know how much I cared. I couldn't bring myself to say the words for some reason, but I knew I loved him.

Curling up next to him on the plush sofa cushions, I drifted off into a restful, dreamless sleep. He nudged me awake about an hour and a half later. I opened my eyes to see him standing over me, tray of snacks in hand. This man might be my favorite person on the face of the Earth. Or any other realm.

“It probably won't be long now, so I thought we'd eat before you go.”

“You know me so damn well. One of the many reasons I adore you.”

We ate, then Xavier came to join us so they could prep me for the meeting with the dragons. Taryk adjusted my outfit, and Xavier brought me my tiara. I asked whether I should bring the baubles Yuri had picked from the vault. We may have not traveled anywhere to need them yet, but I had them.

“Yes. It never hurts to offer a gift, especially since we need so much help from them.”

I used the opportunity to practice my magic, calling them to me from the room upstairs. It had always been one of my easiest skills, but I hadn't been doing much magic at all lately, and I wanted to.

Realizing I needed to let Topaz and Jewel know I would be away, I reached out through the bond. “I will be away from the castle for a couple hours. You will have a guard standing watch, and you will still be able to reach me via the bond. I am only a portal away at any time."

Topaz came across calm and assured. "*Thank you. We will be fine here. Please don't worry about us.*"

"Xavier can you please put a guard or two to watch over Jewel and Topaz? And please, keep Solomon away from them, wherever he is. Oh! Will one of you wear or hold Celeste's bracelet please?"

"How about I take her to the ward room and adjust things so she is able to roam anywhere within them? Then we will only need the bracelet when we travel."

"That would be fantastic. Thank you."

He nodded. And before we could talk about anything else Yuri sang through loud and clear.

"Are you ready? We are here."

Nerves shot through, and I spent a few precious seconds trying to think of a way to back out gracefully. But a hug from Xavier and Taryk's chaste kiss on my forehead gave me the strength I needed.

"Ready."

Closing my eyes, I felt along our bond and pulled the image she sent me. Asking the ring to give me the power I needed, I opened the portal, then my eyes. I had made it directly in front of myself, one step and I was through. Yuri traded me places, waving.

"You'll do great. Don't worry!"

With a deep breath, I let the portal close, and I found myself in a strange land, with nobody I trusted by my side. About to meet a dragon.

I took in my surroundings. We stood at the base of a tree that would have been thousands of years old if it were on Earth. The trunk was massive, the bark dark and solid. I could smell the woodsy scent coming from all directions, and the trees above were so dense that no sunlight found its way to us. All around us, I heard nothing.

"We are well within our wards here, and you are safe. But I request we hurry, so the meeting can take place." Banli seemed to be watching every direction at once, in spite of asserting we were protected.

He turned and descended a set of stairs that I would swear on my life had not been there mere seconds before. I saw no light source, but the passageway held just enough illumination for me to see where I stepped. The stairs spiraled down a very long time, and I followed him mindlessly. I took a brief moment to let Taryk and Xavier know I had safely reached Banli, then turned my attention back to my surroundings.

While I couldn't put my finger on it exactly, something about my surroundings left me feeling unsettled. It may have been that I had never left the safety of a place I knew alone. I'd gone from being alone constantly in my house on Earth, to always having somebody by my side since I entered the cabin. Whatever had triggered it, I didn't like the feeling one iota.

We followed the winding staircase down, farther down than any of the dungeons I had entered thus far. As we reached the end of the long set of stairs, we entered a tunnel. Carved entirely out of the rock, it was bathed in dim light.

I heard my footsteps echo as we walked, but I may as well have been walking alone, because Banli made no sound. My own breaths seemed loud to my ears, and I had the eerie feeling that something watched me from just out of sight. Trying to keep my nerves under control, I dug my fingernails into the palms of my hands. I got an absurd comfort from knowing that when I finally opened my hands to look at my palms there would be tiny crescent-shaped indentations there.

At some point, I began to hear the trickle of running water in the distance. The sounds gave me peace, and for some reason calmed me considerably. Perhaps it had been the total silence aside from the noise of my own making that triggered my discomfort.

All at once, the tunnel opened into a huge cavern. I gasped at the sheer perfection of it. If I had thought the control room at the castle was beautiful, it paled in comparison to the scene before me. Not only did huge crystals cover the walls and dome-shaped ceiling, but a small waterfall cascaded from near the top of the far wall, running through the room and disappearing out the other side.

The room itself had caught my attention so completely that I did not notice the dragon until its voice rang out. Taking a deep breath, I turned to face it.

Giving a respectful bow, I greeted him. Or her. I couldn't tell. The body looked to be the size of a semi truck and covered in gorgeous teal scales. The eyes were filled with sorrow, and the knowledge of an old soul.

“My apologies. The beauty of your home stunned me. I thank you sincerely for the invitation to join you here.”

"Welcome, Princess of Amarys and reigning Chosen Scribe. We are honored you agreed to grant us an audience."

I smiled a genuine smile. "The pleasure is all mine." Since I hadn't been eaten yet, I had begun to feel a little more at ease.

"My name is Marina. My brother Atlas and the young Luna are the only two others of our kind in this realm, as far as we know. I am aware that you request our assistance. As I'm sure you were also told, we desperately need yours."

The tone of her voice tugged at my heart strings in a way that I couldn't describe. "I will do anything I can to help you. We will all be better off when the dark mage is defeated."

"When she began to siphon the magic from the realm, all who lived here were concerned. Creatures became afraid to leave their homes, as many times they would go out and never return. For years, she kidnapped any creature with magic powers and sucked the life out of them. Eventually there became such an imbalance that the universe quit working the way it should."

My heart broke for her, and I could see the sorrow on her face as she told the story. Her sadness created a vibration upon the very air I breathed.

"Babies of all races were born with no magic, even if their parents had possessed some. Plants that had magical medicinal properties stopped curing ailments. The few of our eggs that did manage to hatch left us with sickly babies that did not survive more than a few weeks. Then the eggs stopped hatching at all. The mage somehow managed to capture some of the dragons, who perished when their magic had been depleted. Others simply wasted away. I'd like to think some escaped, but I have no indication that any actually did."

Her deep sigh caused her entire body to tremble with the weight of her sadness. Stretching out her long neck, she rested her elegant head on the floor near where I stood, and I sank to the ground next to her.

"When my mate disappeared, Atlas and I decided it was time to go into hiding. I have two eggs of my own in the clutch that did not hatch. The forest gnomes have been one of the few species we regularly communicated with, and they assisted us to this place.

"We moved all the eggs we could find in hopes that we would be able to keep them safe, and once magic is restored to the lands they may hatch and grow strong. Luna was guarding one of the last ones we found. Her parents had disappeared. She hid alone and terrified, and the egg was all she had left. We brought her here with us, and that marked the last time we left this cave."

"I am so very sorry." I hesitated, unsure if I should share my story with her, but in the end decided I needed to. Everything poured out, the words practically entangling with each other. I never even recognized that I cried even though my tears dripped down on to my hands, folded in my lap.

She wrapped herself around me, drawing me close. We shared the pain of loss, and the uncertainty of what lie ahead. Once the sobs had subsided, I felt silly for ever having been afraid.

Taryk must have felt my distress, as he reached out across the bond to check in with me. I assured him he didn't need to worry, and he silently sent comfort before withdrawing.

"You can communicate telepathically with others?" The teal dragon seemed stunned by this. I didn't understand how she knew, but I saw no reason to lie to her. She probably would have known if I had anyway.

"Yes. I can see the soul threads. If I wish, I can use them to create a bond between myself and another. It allows us to communicate, and I can get a feeling for their whereabouts as well."

"That is impressive for a creature of your race. Very few humans can do such a thing."

"I seem to have many rare qualities. I think they are in part due to my lineage on both sides. My father collected magical abilities for me from those willing to share them, and then passed them on to me at his death. I think, although I am not positive, that the bonding is a result of my scribe heritage, and my ability to see the threads."

She raised her head to my eye level and stared into my soul. "You are an extremely rare and special soul, Everleigh. As a dragon, I have a gift for seeing such things. You will save us all."

I laughed nervously. "No pressure, right?"

"I'd like for you to meet Atlas and Luna, and then we will discuss what we can do to help you prepare for this war."

"I would be honored to meet them."

She moved with a grace the belied her massive size, turning and leading me down a tunnel at the back of the room, just off where the waterfall spilled from the stones. About halfway down, she stopped, gesturing off to her left with a wing.

"Would you like to see the nursery?"

Speechless that she would offer me such a gift, I nodded. She blew gently on the wall and a large doorway appeared.

"Go ahead." She moved to the side to allow me access, and I approached the opening slowly. Peeking around the edge of the wall, the sight almost made my heart stop. There must have been over thirty eggs in there.

"Oh my..." Each sat cushioned in an individual nest. They varied in size, although all would definitely be classified as large from an egg standpoint. The represented every color in the rainbow, either opalescent or shimmering. It was a sight to behold.

"Here lie forty-four potential new dragonettes. Perhaps more if there are any sets of twins, which is rare for us, but not unheard of. Our dream is to help you help them live."

I gazed at her for a moment. "May I ask which two are yours?"

She looked off to the left, and two eggs near the wall began to glow softly. One of them significantly larger than the other, they were both beautiful shades of silvery white. They were the only two that exhibited no other coloration.

I walked over to their nests, kneeling next to them. "May I touch them?"

"Yes, our eggs are quite sturdy."

I extended my hand, and lightly made contact with the shell of the larger egg. It was both hard and leathery at the same time. While the exterior was sleek and smooth, almost like suede, you could also feel the protective inner layer that made the shell almost impenetrable. Leaning in, I rested my forehead against the egg and closed my eyes.

I inhaled deeply, noting the scent echoed that of rainwater and thunderclouds. I called up my sight, not sure what, if anything, would become visible to me. To my surprise, two tiny tapestries became visible immediately. I gasped. They were pale, and not fully colored, but I could feel their strength. These little lives wanted a chance.

Moving my hands to the second egg, I easily pulled a single tapestry into view. This baby appeared to be more fully developed than its siblings. The colors of the threads were saturated and strong. I wondered if I could give him or her enough magic to hatch?

Removing my hands, I turned to Marina. "Would they thrive if they were to hatch now? Do they need the outdoors, or a consistent influx of magic for their growth and health?"

She looked surprised at my questions. Her scaly brows lifted, then furrowed together. "To be honest, I cannot say. The outdoors, not so much until they need to learn to fly, which happens after a few weeks. I assume if one could give them enough magic to hatch then we would also need to continually feed them magic until they grew strong enough to produce their own."

“I apologize if my questions are painful. I admit I do not know enough about dragons to assume even the basics.”

She bobbed.. “My babies, are they healthy? Do you think they will make it?”

I didn't feel comfortable making a statement such as that, but I couldn't very well refuse to tell her anything. “I can tell you that this egg,” I indicated the smaller of the two, “is very strong. His or her tapestry is vibrant and solid. The other egg,” pointing to the larger one, “is very special. The egg contains two babies.”

She inhaled sharply. “Twins? But are they doing okay?”

“I will be honest, I am no dragon doctor. Their coloring is less vibrant, but that may be because they are sharing the magic right now. Both look whole with no weak spots in the threads, and seem to be stable.”

Crystalline tears fell from her eyes. She nudged me gently with her head. “I cannot thank you enough.”

“We do not have the time now, but I would like to come back and take a look at all the eggs, if that is okay with you? I think that when I have more knowledge about dragons in general, I can make a more educated assessment.”

“You are welcome here at any time. I will grant you access to visit whenever you choose. Let’s meet the other two. The sooner we destroy the dark mage, the sooner we can live our lives. I would give anything to be able to soar through the sky once more.”

She led the way down the remainder of the tunnel into another large cavern. This one, too, had walls of crystal but was even larger than the first. And no river ran through it.

The dark green dragon settled in the very center of the room made Marina look petite by comparison. He also looked ridiculously grumpy. Straightening my shoulders, I did everything I could to hide the fact that I had gotten nervous again. I was positive he could tell but was polite enough not to call me on it.

"Atlas, meet Everleigh. Everleigh, my brother." He blinked at me but did not utter a single word. Fabulous. He hated me already. I guess as long as he didn't eat me...

"Luna? Can you come here, please?" From behind the great green body a much smaller silver one emerged. Approximately the size of a large horse, her youth was evident in her demeanor.

I turned to face her slowly, smiling gently as I did. "Hi, Luna. I am Everleigh. Thanks for coming out to meet me."

She stopped about ten feet from me and stared. I did my best to meet her gaze, in spite of feeling like my very soul was being tested for its worthiness. I must have passed, because she began to inch closer, stopping close enough that if she extended her neck she could reach me.

"Are you the one?" Her voice rose barely above a whisper.

Looking to Marina for guidance, I'm sure my confusion showed on my face. Gently, Marina told her, "We believe so. And we are doing everything we can to help her."

Luna nodded in a manner wise beyond her years. “Give her my stone.”

The green head jerked up off the ground where it had been resting. “WHAT?” His voice echoed throughout the cavern, even gruffer than I had imagined it would be. “No.”

It was a statement, and his tone left zero room for argument. Expecting the shy younger dragon to acquiesce, I stared at her, dumbfounded, when she stood up to him.

“It is MINE. And she needs it. So she will have it.”

My head swiveled between the three of them, curious about this stone that obviously had something very special about it. I chose not to say a word, waiting instead for one of them to address me directly.

Marina finally broke the staring contest the two of them were having. “Atlas, she is correct, and I agree with her. If we do not give every aid we can render to those fighting the dark mage, we can expect to stay here in these caverns forever. And there is no guarantee we won't be found as her evil grows stronger.”

“The only other time a human has ever wielded a dragon stone the results were disastrous.”

“Yes. But that is what it will take to be victorious. Do not sentence the realms to disaster because of past mistakes. Use the lesson learned to right the first wrong.”

He looked at me suspiciously, and I got the impression he searched my soul for answers. He sat silently for a long minute, while the three of us stared back at him. At one point he and Marina locked eyes, and I wondered whether they could communicate telepathically.

Luna fidgeted, seemingly on the verge of interrupting. I had reached the decisions to say "Thanks, but no thanks," when he returned his gaze to me.

Marina nodded her head, and Atlas sighed deeply. "Come to me, Princess, and let me tell you about the dragon stones, and how the dark mage gained her power."

Chapter Sixteen

My fist closed reverently around the stone that looked like a tiny version of a dragon's egg. I had wiped the tears from my cheeks and said my goodbyes. I had reached out to let Taryk and Xavier know I would be returning momentarily. And I had memorized the story of the dark mage's beginning so I could return and tell the others.

Standing at the tunnel which would lead back to the tree in the forest, I turned and gave one last wave. Luna stood near the waterfall, watching me go. I had traded the gemstones I brought with me for the dragon stone. It had not been necessary, as she wished to give it to me either way, but because I had them, I felt right giving them to her.

"Thank you, Luna. I will be back soon."

"Go, and be careful."

I held the stone tightly and called on the ring. Its power amplified by the dragon stone, I had no trouble opening a portal into the great hall of the castle and walking though.

Giving Luna one last wave, I allowed it to close behind me and sank down on the sofa.

The visit has lasted only a few hours, but my emotions were drained, and my heart lay heavy. The story Atlas had shared with me gave insight into his gruff demeanor, and apparent distaste for humans. Taryk appeared with a snack, and Xavier let me know he would be returning from the edge of wards momentarily.

I had been attempting to process all the information I had received while in their den, but the dragons had much to share and my brain was on overload. I munched mindlessly on whatever food Taryk had placed before me as we waited for my brother. I only wanted to relay the story once, and then we needed to push forward.

Xavier looked disheveled as he came into view, and I worried about him. "Is everything all right with you?"

He gave me a half smile. "Yes. Preparing for war is exhausting work. As I'm sure you are beginning to notice."

"Ha! Maybe just a little. I have so much to tell you. Celeste are you listening? And is Yuri here?" I looked around but saw nobody.

Celeste manifested as Taryk handed me back the bracelet. We had agreed that we one of us needed to keep it handy at all times, just in case we needed to leave at a moments notice. "Good to see you, my child. I trust the meeting went well?"

“Very.” I only got the single word spoken before Yuri came in from the garden.

“Ah, I see you did not get eaten. Or even lightly toasted. Somewhat a pity, as you could use a tan.”

I pretended to swat at her as she sat on the arm of the sofa beside me. “No. No snack, no toasting, no tan. But I return with much information, and a priceless gift.”

Reaching into my jacket, I removed the stone and held it in the palm of my hand. The light that emanated from it softly created a halo effect, and tiny prisms reflected from its surface. Multiple sharp breaths were taken, which led me to assume most of them knew exactly what I had been given.

“You must protect it at all costs! No one else should even know you have it.”

I returned it to my pocket. “Precisely. Which is why I will be asking Xavier and Taryk to do me a monumental favor. I have already spoken with the dragons about it, and they agreed it would be both safe and prudent.”

Both of the men looked at me suspiciously. “I don't like the sound of this already.” Taryk sat silently waiting while Xavier prodded me for information.

“I need the two of you to work together, to put me under and sew the stone beneath my rib cage.”

Both of them started protesting at the very mention of it, but I hushed them.

"Stop. Listen to me. Marina has already blessed the stone to attune it to me. Inside my body is the only place it will be both safe and hidden. It will continuously power my magic in a way nothing else can. It will also protect me from much of the harm that would come to me while we battle."

Celeste looked thoughtful. Both the guys looked skeptical. Yuri seemed unfazed.

"Between the two of you, the entire procedure will be over in minutes. Thanks to my scribe heritage, I will be one hundred percent healed within a couple hours of waking up. At that point, we will begin returning magic to those who have lost theirs. Once the army is prepared, we will return to the tunnels where I saw my mother and bring the entire crystal box back to the castle."

As much as I wanted to rescue her first, both of the wise dragons advised against it. They explained that using the magic of the dragon stone to rescue her would without a doubt draw the attention of the dark mage, and we needed to ensure we were fully prepared before doing that.

Now, I had to explain to them why. "The reason she is so powerful is because she also possesses a dragon stone. It is a lesser stone than the one I currently have, but she has one, nonetheless."

Every other face in the room looked shocked by the information. Varying degrees of disbelief also showed through.

"What?"

"How?"

"Impossible."

I waited for them to quiet before continuing. "Once, she was a friend to the dragons. Atlas and Marina's father, to be precise. The short version of the story is that he allowed her access to the stone to help her gain control of her magic. She, too, was powerful but untrained at one time. When she felt she could get away with it, she stole the stone and disappeared. They believe she hid it, and only visited it when it was safe to do so, in order to recharge from it."

The similarities in our beginnings haunted me. I had been hesitant to take Luna's stone, even for a good cause. It had been Atlas to explain to me that without the power from another dragon stone, my chances of beating her were slim, even with the specialized weapons from beneath the castle.

"Because she stole it and it was not blessed for her use, the amount of power she can draw from it is limited, and she could never do with that stone what I am proposing to do with this one. At best, she will be able to carry it in a pocket or hold it in her hand. This will give us the chance to separate it from her, while I will have one no matter what."

"I don't not like this one bit." Taryk had scooted close to me on the couch and laid his hand over mine. "It's dangerous."

I met his eyes. "I know. But so is allowing her to continue. And so is attempting to beat her without the stone. Trust me, please. I know we can do this."

Xavier stood. "If we are going to do it, let's get on with it. There is a clinic in the east wing we can use."

I stood too while Taryk remained seated. Xavier looked at him.

"I can do it alone, if you prefer. I understand how hard it would be to cut open the one you love."

Taryk got to his feet. "No, but thank you. What kind of partner am I if I can't be by her side through the hard times? Plus, I will anchor her if there are any complications."

I witnessed the conversation like they had forgotten my presence. It gave me an insight into their relationship, and their support for me. With the two of them on my side, I felt as if the world had my back.

Yuri opted to wait it out. "Sorry, Your Highness, blood and guts is one of my least favorite sights."

"And you, Celeste? Stay or come?" She decided to join us, just in case.

Xavier led the way, and Taryk clutched my hand. His palm stuck to mine, thanks to the sweat that covered it. I could feel his heart beating twice as fast as usual. Considering he usually needed to calm me, it felt a little strange to be on the opposite side of the coin for now.

We entered the clinic, and Xavier began giving instructions. I headed off to put on a gown while the two of them prepped the room. Since most of the "procedure" would involve magic, they simply needed to wash their hands—no way were they putting their dirty ones inside my body, magic or not—and get started.

I lay on the gurney while Xavier gathered the last of the supplies, and Taryk held my hand tightly.

"You know I am going to be fine, right?"

He kissed my knuckles gently. "I know. But we are getting down to the wire, and I know at some point I will not be able to protect you better than you will be able to protect yourself. I will have to step back and let you do what you were born to do. And while I have every faith that you will be victorious, it will still kill me to watch you because I know at some point you will be hurt."

My heart swelled. This man cared so much for me, he didn't want me to be hurt, but also had such faith in me he would let me do it without even trying to argue. For the first time, I took a moment to look toward the future and imagine what our lives might be like when we settled down and lived normally. It certainly gave me something to cling to.

"Ready?" I nodded. "Okay, close your eyes and count backward. You'll be asleep in seconds. I am going to make a single incision and tuck it up under your ribs as you asked. Then I will place magic in there to protect and heal. I will close the wound and wake you after a few minutes. Easy peasy."

"Lemon squeezy?"

After a brief laugh, I began my count down. I started at ten, and don't remember making it past eight.

"Ev... hi." Taryk's face was the first thing I saw upon waking. "How do you feel?"

I blinked at him a couple times, taking an assessment. “Fine. I feel fine, actually.” I tried to sit up.

“Wait just a second. You may feel fine, but there is still a wound that could split open. You are not healed yet. Let me help you a little.”

I went from lying, to sitting, to standing with very little discomfort. I felt the area gingerly. It didn't feel as big as I had expected it to, whether I had already healed some, or he just made it as tiny as possible.

“Thank you. Both of you.”

As I dressed, I remembered to be thankful the incision was above the waistband of my pants. That would have been uncomfortable. I wanted to get started on the army at once, but Xavier convinced me to wait and heal while he gathered those who had volunteered so far.

Yuri headed off with Xavier to get the word out to her people, who had agreed to assist us with relaying messages to the ones who needed to meet us at the castle. Taryk settled me on the couch with Celeste and more food while he went to help with preparations. Once we began returning magic to the residents of the realm, they had to stay within the confines of the wards to prevent the dark mage from feeling the sudden influx of new magic. We certainly didn't want her paying us a visit before we had prepared. Or before I got my mother here.

Marina had explained that the dragon stone would allow me to give magic in the same way my scribe heritage always had. The difference was that I would not be depleted as I did so. The stone would help my magic continuously regenerate, eliminating the need to stop for hours or days at a time until I had enough juice in the tank to give more of myself to the next few.

I palpated the area gently. While still sore, it seemed to be almost completely healed. I could just feel the stone if pushed hard enough up under my ribs. It remained tender though, so I didn't play with it too much. Such an odd feeling, having a foreign body sewn into me. However, I knew without a doubt that I had made the safest decision.

Celeste and I went over the process of restoring magic to the soul of a living being numerous times, and I felt confident I could do it, no problem. I might be slow at first, but it seemed to be a reasonably straightforward process.

I dozed off a little as I waited for the first group to arrive. Celeste remained and hovered silently, watching over me. I caught snippets of the dream state, but since I didn't slip into a deep sleep, I didn't get a good grasp on whatever it had been trying to show me. Hopefully it could wait a bit longer. I sent out a silent prayer to the universe that my mom would still be there when we went to collect her.

Xavier announced via our bond that he would be arriving with the first group momentarily, and I met him in the library. We had previously decided that room made the most sense, as we could close ourselves in with individuals, but it had a large waiting room right outside the doors. It also had a pair of doors leading out to the grounds where we had set up temporary living arrangements. We had done the best we could in the small amount of time we had.

Everyone coming had supposedly been briefed and knew what to expect. I hadn't seen Solomon, and I hoped that continued to be the case, but I knew he had been working on recruiting volunteers, so I wouldn't be too surprised if he made an appearance at some point.

Xavier ushered in the first group and introduced me to the crowd. Nobody seemed to want to be the first guinea pig, even after I assured them that I was indeed the reigning scribe. Everyone throughout the realms knew of the scribe, and her powers. I thought there may have been some seeds of doubt about whether I had the abilities that had been making the rounds in rumors since we began our recruitment process.

Finally, a young fae volunteered. Not only did he agree to step up and be the first to have his magic restored, he also agreed to let the others observe. I almost made a snarky comment about the young one having the only balls in the room but bit my tongue. No sense in alienating those who had come to help us. Although, many of them may have just come because I represented their only chance at getting their magic back. Either way, I decided to play nice. For now.

“What is your name?” I intended to try my best to create a relationship with every one. If they were going to be fighting in our army, I wanted them to know who they were fighting alongside.

We knew everyone we ran across would be willing to fight the dark mage. She had created herself a vast assortment of enemies. What I hoped to accomplish was a group that fought not only against her, but *for* us. Especially here in the kingdom my brother would be ruling.

“D'Mitri, Chosen.” He gave a low bow.

“Please, call me Everleigh. Go ahead and have a seat.” I indicated the chair we had placed in the center of the room.

He sat down rather gingerly as if he half expected it to swallow him whole before we even started. After a second, he scooted back and looked slightly more comfortable.

I took the time to explain to him, and the entire room, what would happen during the process. Thanks to Celeste, I knew that I needed to find the runes in their tapestry and “refill” them. She had explained to me that because their magic had been drained, and not stripped from them, the runes would still be visible, and I basically needed to replenish them. I hoped desperately my intuition would kick in and allow me to do it right on the first try.

“Your only job in the process is to sit here and relax. I am going to place my hand on your shoulder, in the interest of creating a physical connection as well as a magical one, and I will restore your magic. You will have precisely the skills and abilities you had before. You will barely feel the process at all, and there certainly will be no discomfort.”

A young female near the front raised her hand. “Go ahead.” I nodded at her.

“I'm sorry to interrupt, Chosen, but may I ask how this works? Why are you able to return our magic? I was under the impression it was gone forever.”

“What is your name?”

“I'm sorry, I am Endryl.”

“No need to apologize, Endryl. It's nice to meet you. As a soul scribe, one of my responsibilities is to balance magic within the universe. When she drained your magic, she created an imbalance that naturally looks to right itself. In very simple terms, I will use my own magic to refill yours. Are there any other questions?"

From near the back, "How many of us will you be able to return magic to before you run out?"

"In the interest of being honest, I am unsure. However, I know I am capable of manifesting large amounts at a time. I will help as many of you in one session as I can, then rest to replenish myself. I will continue until you all are returned to your former magical states."

After I answered the other questions that arose, it was time to get started. The expressions in the crowd ran from skeptical to curious, and all eyes followed my every move. D'Mitri made every attempt to look relaxed in the chair, but I could feel the waves of nervousness emanating from him. I smiled reassuringly and laid my hand on his shoulder. The contact caused him to startle slightly, but he did not pull away.

Closing my eyes, I pulled his tapestry into view. The sight of it shocked me, and I bit my cheek to keep from gasping out loud.

Chapter Seventeen

I easily found the runes, and their condition left me in shock. She hadn't just drained them to empty. It looked as if she had torn them out. The edges were ragged and the fabric around them had weakened runs through it, reminding me of the tights I wore as a little girl. I needed to both refill and repair each.

Taking a deep breath, I began. In spite of the dragon stone, the task would prove monumental if they were all in the same state. Seeing that time was of the essence, the best I could do was pray that not all of them were as degraded as D'Mitri's.

I followed my inner voice, patching and repairing until the weak areas had disappeared completely. Focusing my power on his empty runes, I pushed the magic from myself into his soul. I could feel the pull as his runes greedily drank the magic in. As water restored the parched

Earth, so the magic rehabilitated his soul.

The colors returned to their vibrant tones, and the runes themselves practically glowed. I allowed the magic to continue pouring into him until the flow slowed, then stopped, of its own accord.

Opening my eyes and removing my hand from his shoulder, I nodded at him. “It is done.”

I watched as he attempted to use his magic for the first time since it had been stolen. I saw the concentration furrow his brow, then watched his eyes go wide as he accessed the innate part of himself that had been missing for so long.

He jumped to his feet, throwing his arms around me with laughter. “Chosen, forgive me my forwardness, but I cannot thank you enough. I admit I had doubts, but I was wrong!”

Murmurs ran through the small group we had assembled. Some still sat with their brows raised, but many wore smiles. D'Mitri made his way out the doors into the garden to spread the word that I could, indeed, restore their magic.

Taryk joined us in the library, taking a seat at the edge of the room to watch. Seven more cycles, all needing varying levels of repair, and then Endryl stood alone. “Are you ready?” I asked her.

“May I speak with you first, Chosen, if you have the time?” She wrung her hands and looked nervously at the men.

“Of course. I will make the time. Will you boys give us a minute?”

Xavier and Taryk stepped out to the garden, mingling with those wandering around the grounds. We sat on the couch, sided by side, and I turned to Endryl and smiled, hoping to encourage her.

“Well, when the dark mage drained my magic, I was expecting a baby. I never gave birth, but also never lost the baby. Everything just kind of stopped. My spouse didn't make it. The draining of his magic cost him his life.”

Tears slipped silently down her cheeks. She didn't bother to wipe them away, but kept her hands pressed to her belly. My heart broke for her.

“I guess what I am trying to say, is that I do not know how having my magic restored will affect me, or the baby, if he or she is somehow still there.”

I thought of the dragon eggs. They did not perish when magic disappeared, they simply stopped growing and progressing. I assumed it would be the case here but couldn't be sure.

“May I touch you and use my sight to see if there is another soul within you? It will give us an idea of how to proceed.”

She nodded, and I held out my hand. Grasping her fingers in mine, I closed my eyes. Her soul touched me immediately with its beauty in spite of the ragged tears where her magic had been drained. Widening my scope, I searched for the second soul.

Just as I began to give up hope, I found it. Tiny and wan, it presented almost as a patch upon Endryl's own soul, layered over and connected, yet individual. I pushed a tiny amount of magic toward it, almost as an offering, and it was absorbed immediately. Opening my eyes, I saw her worried face.

"Your baby waits for you. It is nestled within you, and immediately accepted the magic I offered. I believe if we restore your power that he or she will continue to grow as if there had never been an interruption. Whether I do that or not will be entirely up to you."

Silent tears turned to sobs. I wrapped my arms around her and held her close, letting her have her moment. To be so young, she had suffered so much. Taryk caught my eye as he watched through the glass doors. I smiled at him and let him know there was nothing for him to worry about.

Her sobs subsided and I could feel her attempting to gather her composure. Wiping the tears from her cheeks, she looked at me. I could feel her distress, and her uncertainty weighed on me.

"Is it safe? What would I be condemning my baby to if I give birth during these times?"

"I cannot make any guarantees. But I will offer you this. You are welcome to take refuge here in the castle. If you wish to accept the return of your magic now, and bring your baby into this world, we will do everything we can to protect you. This is the safest place you could possibly be. Will the war come to our doorstep? Possibly. I don't believe these wards will be breached. And I do believe we will win the war."

I held her hand as she struggled to make her decision.

"I do not know how long you have until you give birth, but there is a chance the war will be over long before the baby arrives."

She nodded. “I should have about six months left.”

“If all goes well, this war could be over by then. Our hopes are to prepare as best we can, then strike fast and catch her off guard. But I do not want you to feel pressured. I can return your magic at any time. It does not have to be done now.”

“But you need my magic. That is why I came. I am a healer. In times of war, I can be an invaluable help.”

“No. We want you safe. We want your baby safe. Even if I return your magic, I would not want you to endanger yourself now. If you elect to receive your magic, I would still want you to stay within the castle wards where you are safe. If we need your assistance it will be to heal those that are here. I will not allow you to go into battle and endanger what will be the first birth here in a very long time. I believe you will better serve us as an ambassador of hope. Show the people that life is returning, and that we will be victorious.”

Endryl smiled. “An ambassador of hope. I like the sound of that. I am ready.”

I motioned Taryk to return, and after asking permission, explained the situation.

“Congratulations. And welcome. I know you will be happy here in the castle.”

I grabbed her hand again. “Ready?”

At her nod, I closed my eyes and pulled forth her runes. I paid special attention to every last thread, ensuring there would be no complications in growing a healthy baby. The tapestry of the young, while wan and almost colorless, appeared to be whole.

It was here I focused the magic first. The tiny being drank it in as if it had been parched. I fed and fed, until I had to pull away for a break. I couldn't understand why it did not fill completely.

Looking at Taryk, I explained my problem via our bond. After a moment, he nodded. I looked sharply at Endryl when I heard her gasp. Her belly had grown considerably.

"You must return her magic first. The babe is using everything you are giving it to grow, instead of slowly growing off his or her mother's reserves."

I met her eyes. "I am so, so sorry. I did not know how magical babies grow and develop."

Before she could answer me, I closed my eyes again, and focused. In the moments we had been discussing the situation the small tapestry had already lost some of the color it had gained. I fed magic into Endryl's runes. I let her soul drink from mine as it refueled itself. I left the floodgates open, allowing both of them to draw from me as needed. When the transfer of power finally ebbed, I felt unsteady, but thrilled. Both of their tapestries were vibrant and alive.

Opening my eyes, I saw Taryk watching me with concern. I gave him a reassuring look and turned to face Endryl.

Her eyes were wide, and wonder filled her features. Both her hands lay on her rounded belly, and she sat silent and motionless for the next few moments. Finally, her eyes met mine, and she grinned.

“I cannot thank you enough, Chosen. You have no idea what this means to me.”

“Please, call me Everleigh. I think you and I are going to be great friends. And I apologize that I may have taken away some of your six-month timeline.”

“Do not apologize. You have returned things to me that I never believed I would have again. I have nothing but gratitude for all you have done for me, and all that you are doing for the rest of us. Without you, we would be waiting for the dark mage to triumph and enslave us all. You have given us a chance, and most importantly, hope.”

We embraced, and I sent word to Xavier that I would like to give her a room within the castle. He offered the room on the landing next to mine, or one of the suites in the east wing, a choice I passed along to her.

“Do you mind if I room next to you? I feel more comfortable next to someone I've at least met.”

“Absolutely, let's get you settled in. Where are the items you brought with you?” I requested Xavier's presence as we headed out of the library.

He met us head on as we exited through the doors to the yard, and I introduced them.

“Endryl, this is my brother, Xavier, and the crown prince of Amarys. Xavier this is Endryl.”

I hid a smile as I watched Xavier's eyes linger, and his best grin emerge. “Nice to meet you, Endryl. Welcome to our home.”

She blushed and thanked him. The two stood staring at each other silently while I was content to watch whatever seed had just been planted between them. Whatever it would lead to would be blooming soon, if their reactions to each other were any indication.

Solomon chose that moment to come striding into the yard and demand Xavier's attention. I swallowed a peevish expression, letting Xavier know we would see him later, and turned to go.

"Wait!" We turned back to him. "Endryl, if you are not otherwise engaged, perhaps you would like to have dinner with me this evening?"

Solomon interjected before she even had a chance to answer, and the shock on her face showed.

"He doesn't have time for a dinner date. He has work to do."

I didn't have time to open my mouth before Xavier put him in his place. "You are not responsible for *my plans,* cousin. It would be best if you not only remembered your place but took a more gracious attitude toward *my* guests."

Turning his back fully on Solomon, he smiled at Endryl. "My apologies. The invitation stands, and I would love to dine with you. I will make the time, if you are agreeable."

She nodded shyly, looking down to attempt to hide the blush staining her cheeks.

"Thank you. I will see you this evening." His smile for Endryl disappeared as he turned to face his cousin. "Now, what can I do for you?"

I could hear the snarky tone in Solomon's reply, but not the words he spoke, and I hoped to high heaven my brother got that insolent ass under control. If he didn't, I would likely do so, probably out of anger. I already knew that would be a disaster. And that assumed Taryk didn't beat me to it.

We collected Endryl's things, and I showed her to the room next to mine. Along the way, I pointed out the bathing room and which door led to my room.

Leaving her to take a nap in her new bed, I caught up with Taryk and Xavier in the library. Both had concerned looks on their faces.

"Uh-oh, now what?" I had no desire for any road blocks. I just wanted to return magic to those who had volunteered, and get my mother from that pit she lay in.

Taryk shook his head. "You cousin. He is a piece of work."

Xavier waved his hand. "I dealt with him. I wish I could say what his problem is, but I honestly have no idea."

"Xavier, can we trust him?"

He shrugged. "I am beginning to doubt his allegiance. Keep your eyes open at all times. I hate to think he would betray us, but I have concerns. Let Yuri and Celeste know when you see them, would you?"

I agreed. "I am not comfortable returning his magic to him. I don't think it's a safe move for any of us."

"The odd thing is that he hasn't asked to have his returned. I find it highly suspicious. Normally he is the type that would have jumped on the opportunity. Either way, I will delay him if it comes up."

"Okay, then. Shall we move on with the volunteers?"

We spent the next few hours moving the residents of the castle through the library. It reminded me somewhat of an assembly line. Word of my success earlier had made the rounds, and doused any skepticism, so we didn't have to waste time on answering questions.

Xavier and Taryk ushered them in by groups, and I made a single announcement explaining what would happen for each of them. Then we moved right along. The rest I got between groups and during my short speech seemed to be enough to recharge so that I could continue on.

Twice Xavier left us to usher a new group in through the wards. The crowd of allies grew steadily, but I had the fear it couldn't possibly be enough.

We broke for dinner and agreed to return after eating. Together the decision was made to continue the process as long as we had volunteers willing to come in, and I didn't get too worn out. Every thought running through my head led to collecting that crystal coffin and bringing my mother back to us. The sooner I completed this task, the sooner I could focus on that.

Taryk and I ate a quiet meal alone together. Xavier had gone on his "date" with Endryl, and Yuri had gone to eat with her grandmother. Celeste obviously didn't need to eat, and wandered the castle keeping her eyes and ears open.

We moved to the sofa in the grand hall and looked out at the grounds. I needed to see Jewel and Topaz soon. I checked in regularly via the bond, but always felt better after a visit. I leaned into Taryk's side as I rested and reflected on all that had changed in such a short time.

“How long do you think we have to keep her hidden to satisfy the prophecy?” If there was a hard and fast cut-off time, I knew the dark mage would be appearing at some point before it ended.

“Prophecy is funny like that. None of it is written in stone. The only certain thing is the sooner we defeat her, the sooner we can relax and stop worrying.”

“Ain't that the truth.” I closed my eyes, intending to rest for just a few minutes before we had to return to the library. I'd take my tiny naps wherever I could get them.

The musty smell assaulted my senses, and my eyes jerked open. This time I stood directly in front of the stone table that held the crystal coffin aloft. It lay there, dark and foreboding. I desperately wanted to place my hands on it and bring forth the light, to see my mother’s face and reassure myself she still lay there, but something held me back. Somehow this visit seemed different, but I couldn't pinpoint exactly how.

A feeling of impending disaster filled me. The discouragement felt as if it came from the ground, winding its way over my feet and up my legs. It climbed higher and higher, compressing my torso. I felt my breaths coming in short gasps. All I wanted to do was drop to the ground and give up, but I had no control over my body.

Squeezing my eyes shut, I reached for the dragon stone. I pulled its power into myself, then pushed it outward, at last breaking the hold over me. I sat upright on the couch, Taryk looming over me. Our foreheads cracked, and I collapsed backward. Blinking repeatedly, I gazed up at him.

"You already have one hell of a goose egg on your forehead."

He shook his head wryly. "Yeah? Well, you're bleeding, so you lose."

I reached up gently and pulled my hand away at the sticky wetness. Examining my fingertips, I sighed. He was right. Xavier came from the other room, cloth in hand. Endryl followed.

"I hope I am not intruding."

I laughed, slightly hysterically. "Nope. Welcome to a day in my life."

Chapter Eighteen

The split in my skin had already begun to close by the time they got the blood wiped off. Taryk wanted me to sit and recuperate. I just needed to get the magic returned to the last of the volunteers who were waiting. The urgency to bring my mother back to the castle had grown exponentially. I couldn't nail down the origin of the feeling in the dreamscape, but it lingered like a bad smell.

In spite of their wishes, they followed me reluctantly into the library. Celeste appeared as I waited for the next group.

"It seems your cousin is sowing seeds of discord amongst those gathered here. He is raising questions about whether you can be trusted. He has told some of our volunteers that you are only returning magic to them so they can feed the dark mage once again."

"Damn that childish asshole. I knew he was going to be trouble."

I let Xavier know via the bond that we needed to have a conversation before he brought the next group in, and he appeared almost immediately, closing the door behind him.

Celeste relayed to him the same message she had brought to me moments earlier.

"It's up to you what we do with him, Xavier, but we need to do something." I had no patience for this behavior, and he could ruin our chances for victory before they ever got off the ground.

"I could talk to him again, but I doubt it would have an impact. So our choices are to banish him, or imprison him."

"So, as much as I am against imprisoning people, I am deathly afraid if we banish him that he will seek out our enemy and betray us further. We cannot afford to have her know what we are up to before we are ready."

He sighed, shoulders drooping. "You are right. At least without his magic it will not be an epic battle to imprison him. I will find him now."

"Don't go alone. Find someone to help you. Taryk and I will continue with the current group. Celeste, will you see if you can figure out where he is right now, please? And ask for Yuri's help as well, if she is back."

Celeste nodded and disappeared from sight. Xavier agreed he would get someone we trusted to help. He left and sent the next group in on his way out.

It took me only the next couple of hours to return magic to the remaining volunteers. At this point, we had a small army built up. And by small, I meant approximately three hundred. Without telling anyone else what I was doing, I had added a little something extra to each of the volunteers.

I'd argued with myself about it, knowing that technically it was wrong to change anything about another being without their permission, but I truly believed it could turn the tides in our favor if we found ourselves slipping behind.

In each volunteer, I had left behind a minuscule opening. Should any of them be in need, I would be able to push forth magic to bolster their power. I assuaged my guilt by the knowledge that I could not take from them in any way without their permission, and I had initiated no bond or other invasion of their privacy. I also made sure that the opening would only accept my own magic, nobody else could influence them in any way.

Since the bond did not exist to forewarn me, I would have to know some other way that they needed assistance, but I saw this as a last-minute reprieve. If our army looked to be in danger of losing the battle, I could open the floodgates wide and increase our power exponentially.

Sinking to the couch after the last of the volunteers left the room, I looked at Taryk. “We need to bring my mother back here. Tonight.”

“Whoa. I know you are in a hurry, but let’s be sure Solomon is dealt with, and we have a plan in place for the worst-case scenario. We need to proceed carefully in case this is a trap."

"Whether it's a trap or not, I am NOT leaving my mother in that hell hole one second longer than is absolutely necessary."

"I'm not saying we are. But you need to make an honest assessment of what is deemed necessary. All I'm saying is that we need to have everything prepared for whatever might come with that crystal coffin she's in. I highly doubt they put her there like that with no plan in place. We need to have a plan too."

Before I could respond, Xavier came in with Celeste behind him. "We have a problem."

"Of course, we do. Because why wouldn't we?" I leaned my head against the back of the sofa and sighed. "What happened?"

Celeste came to hover near me. "Solomon has disappeared."

"What? How can that be? He has to be within the wards somewhere, right?"

Xavier cleared his throat. "If he is, we don't know where he could be hiding. Yuri is bringing in a team of wood sprites to help us search for him."

"Jewel! We have to protect her."

Reaching out through our bond, I checked in on them. Topaz confirmed it seemed quiet all around, and Jewel slept peacefully. I warned her to be on the highest alert and sent an image of Solomon to her. I let her know that she needed to call me at once if she saw him, or if she felt uncomfortable in any way with anyone who showed up in the stable. As soon as we found a trustworthy guard, I'd be posting more around their stall.

"No matter what, trust no one new until I have verified them. I will come and introduce any new staff to you personally."

She agreed, and I focused once more on Xavier. "Do you think this might have something to do with the fact that he didn't ask for his magic back? Because he still has it?"

"I hope not. That would mean he either somehow eluded her when she was draining magic, which would be okay, or he is in collusion with her and has been all along. Either way, he should not be able to get through the wards..."

"Perhaps our first order of business should be to alter the wards? Can we specify that he specifically is not able to pass either way, no matter what magic he possesses?"

"That's a good idea. I will do it now." He stood to go, and I copied him.

"I want to come too. I have something else I want to discuss with you that involves the wards, so we might as well do it now."

Using the bond, in case there were prying ears about the castle, I explained to Xavier what I had been thinking as we headed for the ward room. We tossed ideas back and forth as we walked, plotting and planning for various scenarios. By the time we reached our destination, we had a fairly solid plan in place.

As we left the ward room, Yuri arrived with her crew. We met them in the tunnels to allow them to cross the wards, and Xavier apprised them of the situation.

Yuri was incensed. “I knew he was a shady, good-for-nothing cretin! If he is here, we *will* find him. Come on, everyone, let's get him.”

She buzzed off with at least forty wood sprites racing after her, each intent on being the one to track the traitor down. Their competitiveness became obvious as they shouted good-natured insults at each other while they zipped up the stairwell.

“Well,” I said wryly, “if he is still here, they will find him!”

As we reached the turn off that led to the other underground hallway, we exited the stairwell, and confused Taryk.

“Wait. Where are you going?”

Oops. I'd forgotten he hadn't been listening in on our conversation and needed to be brought up to speed.

“We have fortified the wards for one of these rooms. It is where we will bring the crystal coffin when we get my mother.”

He sighed. “Ev—”

“Nope. I've talked with Xavier and we have it all settled.”

Now it was Xavier's turn to look confused. “Wait. You didn't discuss it with Taryk? I assumed you two were already on the same page.”

“We are. He just needs to catch up.” I made sure to use a tone that sent the message clearly. I would not be swayed by any argument. This needed to be done, and it needed to be done now.

We stalked down the rest of the hallway in silence. Our plan included minimal fuss and was very straightforward. The room we had chosen sat at the farthest end of this hallway. It had no other access point other than the singular door. It lay deep within the earth for maximum natural protection, and we had seriously beefed up the wards covering every last inch of it.

If we discovered that the crystal coffin did, in fact, come with any sort of magical spells, assaults or funny business, it would be contained to that singular room. We planned to open a portal directly to the room that housed the coffin, pull said coffin into the prepared room, and close the portal. Hopefully in less than thirty seconds. If any sort of hang up came along, we would deal with it.

I could not, in good conscience, leave her to lie in that dark, musty room. Assuming she had been there since the night she appeared to us in the study, when we thought she had died, it had already been too long. Hell, one minute would have been too long, in my opinion.

The three of us stood in the center of the room, making last minute plans. It had no furniture, and we planned to just lay the coffin on the floor. This lessened the chance of anything being used against us, should there be a scuffle of any sort.

Assuming the coffin itself would be extremely heavy we intended to use our magic to bring it through the portal. Taryk had demanded we do it that way so I didn't actually have to set foot in the underground room since we had no idea where it was located. He feared I would get trapped there alone, and they would have no way to attempt a rescue.

I had entertained that same concern while pondering all the ways we could be caught off guard during the rescue attempt and didn't like the thought of taking on the dark mage by myself. As far as I had come, I still had a whole lot to learn. I very much needed the more experienced ones in our group to back me up. I had no doubt that should we engage in a one-on-one battle at this point, I would lose. Sorely. And if I lost? Well, so did every being in every realm. No pressure, right?

Shaking the stiffness and tension from my joints, I took a deep breath. “Are we ready?”

The look on Taryk's face shouted without words that he believed we were making a major mistake. He had tried to clarify his thought process to me earlier, but I had stubbornly refused to hear him out. Part of me felt bad about it, but I couldn't abandon my mother, even for him. In my grown-up brain I knew that wasn't even close to what he had been asking of me, and that he only wanted to keep me safe. Unfortunately the petulant, head-strong teenager in me had been in charge at the time, and I shut him down without really giving him a chance. I'd have to apologize when we had done what I came here to do.

He refused to even nod, another way of showing me he disagreed. The only reason he joined us was to help keep me safe. If he had believed it to be less dangerous, he probably would have gone to sulk in a corner.

Xavier nodded, and I opened myself to the power of the ring.

The wards had been set such that no other could make a portal into or out of this room. The only way for anything bad to get in would be for it to come through the portal I made, either slipping in while it remained open, or hitching a ride on the coffin itself.

We each believed that to be the most likely scenario. I highly doubted she would be placed into a coffin and then left unattended without some serious mojo involved. After all, the scribe magic is what the dark mage lusted after, and the only way for her to get her hands on it would be to find out who had it now.

Expelling the breath in my lungs, I opened a portal directly to the dark room that I had seen the coffin in. Peering through, the darkness allowed us no sight. Taryk powered up an orb of light and sent it in. Sure enough, right where it had been in my dream, lay a crystalline coffin on a stone riser.

Xavier used his magic and called it forth. For a brief moment, it seemed like it wouldn't budge, then it slid through the portal and came to rest on the floor. As soon as Taryk's orb had returned to the room, I closed the connection.

In this light, it looked empty.

"Ev, are you sure..." Taryk's voice trailed off as I shot him a disparaging look.

"Of course, I am sure. Seriously? Watch."

Reaching out, I laid my hand against the casket, waiting for the light to show them her face. Nothing. I frowned. Shifting slightly, I placed both hands against the smooth surface, stunned by how cold it felt. Still nothing.

"Ev..."

"She WAS in there! I saw her. With my own eyes! I am not making this up!" I could feel the hysteria coming on, but I could do nothing about it.

Xavier's voice broke in. "Everleigh, I know how much you wanted this to be true, but I believe we have triggered a trap. We need to try to put the coffin back. Quickly!"

Standing, I opened the portal to what should have been the earthen room with the stone plateau in the middle. A solid wall of dirt met us instead of the view we had been expecting.

"Damn it! What is happening?"

Xavier and Taryk both stood over the coffin, murmuring and working their own magic simultaneously. Spell after spell they cast, attempting to contain whatever evil I had just insisted on inviting into our midst.

For a moment, I just stared, unable to believe she hadn't appeared when I touched it. In spite of the desire to run away and hide, I got to my feet and began helping the guys. Any incantation I knew that I believed would be even remotely helpful I cast over it. Finally each of us cast our own trigger spell, so that we would be instantly alerted if a single breath of magic disturbed the room.

Standing in the hall while I waited for Xavier and Taryk to lay even more magic over the door, the tears began to fall. She had been there, I knew it. I had not been imagining things, even though I had seen her in a dream, I had *seen* her.

I knew her soul still lingered within these realms, or she would have had a statue at the chateau. Unfortunately, this coffin did not contain her essence, and whatever it did harbor had just gained free entry right into the very midst of our safe haven.

What had I done?

Chapter Nineteen

We made the walk back to the library in silence. Sinking into the sofa, I put my head into my hands and cried. She had been in that casket. I *saw* her. And yet it lay in the room below, empty. A harbinger of evil and danger in our very midst. Who could say what horror I had dragged into the castle? I had endangered every being we brought here to be safe.

If it turned out to be a spy of any kind, I may have just given our position and plans away. If it turned out to be a gateway, I may have just opened us all up to attack. I let her prey on my pain, and the cost could be catastrophic for all of us.

Taryk and Xavier paced the room as they discussed contingency plans. We needed to be prepared for every eventuality and we had no time to spare.

Finally, Taryk perched on the edge of the sofa. "Everleigh, I'm sorry she wasn't in there. We will find her."

"But she WAS. I saw her. I did not imagine it. And now I have endangered us all."

"What's done is done. We need to be ready for anything. We need to gather what we can of an army and make our move before she has the chance to learn any of our secrets."

I hung my head in shame. If I had just listened to their requests to slow down and learn everything we could before opening the portal, we wouldn't have been in this position. I wanted to retreat to my room and pull the covers over my head as I had done in my younger years. Although I had long since learned the lesson that ignoring a problem didn't make it go away, it still stood at the top of my list for ways to deal with unpleasantness. Especially if said unpleasantness was my own bloody fault.

One of the guys asked me to call Celeste into the library, and I did so without acknowledging them. As she appeared beside me, they began explaining what had happened and asking her for insight on the situation. I tuned them out and continued to mope silently.

Their muted conversation carried on around me as I pouted. I had ventured so far into my own thoughts that I did not hear them calling my name until Xavier laid his hand on my shoulder, causing me to jerk upright.

"Wha- I'm sorry. Are you talking to me?"

The three of them looked at me wryly. "Have you not been

paying attention my child? I would have assumed you understood that this is a matter of utmost importance?" Celeste hovered directly in front of me.

"Yes. I mean no. Hell. I'm sorry. No, I have not been paying attention, apparently, but I do understand the importance."

"How can you understand the importance of the subject if you weren't even listening to the conversation. We could have been discussing tea leaves for crying out loud!" I could tell my brother's patience had begun to thin when it came to my pity party.

I took a deep breath, exhaling out for as long as I could. Then I did it once more for good measure. "I said I'm sorry. However, I do happen to know that whatever you may have been discussing, it is probably important."

Taryk shot him an exasperated look and sat next to me. "Please stop feeling guilty. We all make mistakes. What matters now is that we get the best grip on the situation possible, which means we need all hands on deck, okay?" He gave my leg a gentle squeeze.

"I know, and I am sorry. I just feel like a failure. I endangered us all."

Xavier laid his hand on my arm and smiled gently. "Let's just do what we can to make smart choices from here on out. That's all we can do for now anyways. Help us make a plan."

And so I did. We plotted and planned to the best of our abilities, using whatever resources we had available to us.

After a while Yuri returned to report that the sprites had been unable to find hide nor hair of the blasted Solomon. Either he had an out-of-this-world hiding place, or he had managed to cross the wards. My bet was on the latter, unfortunately. We hadn't given him any inkling that he needed to be hiding from us.

Yuri agreed to lend some of their warrior sprites to help guard Jewel. Their small size would make them easy to hide, so it would be less obvious that the stall was heavily fortified, should anyone with poor intentions make it that far.

As we walked to the stable, I filled Yuri in on what had happened with the crystal coffin. Instead of blaming, she sympathized with how hard it is to lose a parent, as she had lost both of hers in the early days of the dark mage's time here.

"I can't imagine losing her, then believing you might be able to get her back, just to find out she really is lost. I'm so sorry."

"That's the thing. Her soul is still trapped here somehow. Otherwise, she would have a statue in the Hall of Remembrance back at the chateau. Whether she is truly deceased or not, I cannot say, but either way she needs our help. But I would have bet my own life that she lay in the crystal coffin. I saw her clear as could be."

"Well, as you are learning, magic can play many tricks on our perception. We will help you. She will reach her eternal rest, one way or the other. I promise."

Reaching the stables, I saw Topaz in the door of her stall, looking out toward the fields. I introduced Yuri and the sprites she had brought to watch over them.

"Are you okay? You seem stressed."

"*Something is not right. I can't say exactly what, but there is a disturbance here.*"

I looked out the direction she had been gazing. Closing my eyes, I reached out, hoping to sense whatever she may be feeling. Unfortunately, that area of my skills still needed quite a bit of work. While I could detect other souls in the area, that did us no good since they were everywhere within the castle wards.

"Do you believe they are close? Or do you feel like it may be beyond the wards?" I would take whatever input she might be able to provide.

"*I cannot say. I will continue to monitor the feeling and let you know right away if anything changes.*"

After filling her in on all that I could, I took a peek at the still-sleeping Jewel. She looked so peaceful lying there, blissfully unaware of what went on around her. Knowing and trusting that we would keep her safe, she simply slept.

I walked Yuri to the wards after picking up the remainder of her crew. They would be returning to the outside to bring back one last group of volunteers as large as they could find. With time being of the essence now, we planned to use the small army we had gathered and move forward, rather than try to grow our forces and be caught in an attack unaware.

As we said our goodbyes, I looked her in the eyes. “I wish you were staying here with me.” She had become my close friend, and I wanted her to stay by my side.

“I shall return tomorrow. From then on out, you will not be able to get rid of me no matter how hard you try.” She kissed my forehead gently, then sped off with a jaunty wave.

As I walked down the tunnel and headed for the staircase, I stopped by the door to the only occupied cell.

“How are you doing in there, Angus? Are you getting everything you need?”

“Yes, Chosen. Bored to death, but comfortable.”

“Sorry you are bored. It really shouldn't be too much longer before all of this unpleasantness is over.”

“Glad to hear it.” His solemn tone made me feel bad for him all over again, but there would be no more making impetuous decisions for me. I had already made more than my fair share of wrong ones. And hopefully I told him the truth—there really wouldn't be much more time for him to spend down here before he could go home.

I headed up the stairs, stopping at the midway landing. Reaching out with my senses, I attempted to tell if any magic leaked from the sealed room that held the coffin. The temptation to walk down the hall and open the door made me shudder.

I just wanted to look one more time. I had been so sure that when I placed my hand upon the glass her image would appear once more, and we would find a way to release her from her imprisonment. Other than my own internal struggle, I sensed nothing more in the hall.

Turning to go, I had barely made it up two stairs before all the orbs went dark. The stairwell plunged into inky blackness and I didn't dare move a muscle, trying to pinpoint what had happened. Reaching out via my bonds, I called Taryk, Xavier, and Celeste. They all started my way, but I had no idea if they would reach me before something else did.

I heard Angus hollering down below, wanting to know why I had turned off his lights. Afraid to yell back at him, I stood silently, waiting for the others to appear. It took fewer than two minutes before I heard them calling my name as they made their way down the stairs.

Realizing Angus had gone silent, I wondered if his lights turned back on. Reaching out my hand, I felt for whoever had come down the stairs first.

Whispering, though I didn't know why, I gently called their names. “Taryk? Xavier? Can you light up an orb? I can't see a damn thing.”

“Everleigh... what are you talking about? The lights are already on. We can see just fine.” Xavier sounded puzzled.

“What? It's pitch black in here.”

Taryk grabbed my hand. “I am going to pick you up and carry you out of here. Hold tight.”

As he lifted me into his arms, I buried my head against his chest, dumbfounded. I hadn't been imagining it. I s*till* couldn't see. And Angus had been yelling about the lights as well. Something very strange had happened in this stairwell just now.

"I'm going to see what I can sense," Xavier's voice sounded farther away. "Be right behind you."

"Wait!" I panicked at the thought of him being down here alone. Something wasn't right. "I don't think any of us should be alone down here. Come up with us, and then you and Taryk can come back down."

I could hear that he didn't understand my fear, but he agreed. As we reached the great room and Taryk set me down, I opened my eyes, and could see perfectly. Both of the guys face's stared back at me, concerned.

"We are going back to check out the hallway and be sure the room is still sealed. None of us felt a warning triggered by magic in the vicinity, but something obviously blinded you." Taryk still held tightly to my hand.

"It wasn't just me. When it first got dark, I heard Angus yelling too. Then he got quiet."

"I think," Xavier said quietly, "that we need to get that coffin out of here. It seems able to affect you if you get close enough to it without triggering any of the sensory spells we laid. It's too dangerous to have it here."

"But what if her soul really is attached to it? We can't just send it off and leave her somewhere." The ridiculous fear that I would be abandoning my mother if the crystal box left my possession reared its ugly head. It seemed to make me completely irrational. Taryk tried to gently point that out to me.

"Ev, listen. It's not like we are going to sink it to the bottom of the ocean. We will put it somewhere safe that isn't here. We will lay all the protection we can on it and come back to it when we can. It will be fine, I promise you."

Once again, rational me knew he was right. But irrational me, who happened to be in charge at the moment, was having none of it.

"No."

Xavier leaned over and whispered in Taryk's ear, and he nodded. Grabbing my hand, he pulled me along. "Let's go for a walk, okay?"

Glad of the subject change, I agreed. As we got farther from the stairs, and then out of the castle all together, a fog lifted and my brain seemed to clear. What the hell?

I stopped suddenly, dragging Taryk to a halt as well. "How is that possible?"

He peered into my eyes, searching for something. Satisfied with whatever he saw, or didn't see, he smiled at me gently.

"The dark mage's powers are very strong, and she has had many years to perfect the subtle spells. You are strong as well, and have naturally resistant protections, so the best she can do is try to influence you indirectly and without your knowledge. I believe that is why she began in the dreamscape, because you are most vulnerable there."

The thought caused me to shudder. Now that I could think

clearly, I believed every word he said. We needed to get that thing out of there before she had the ability to affect anyone else in the castle.

He turned us around and headed back to the castle. "Your brother has a plan, and we will get it out of here right now. First, I would like to ask you to trust me."

I nodded. Of course, I trusted him.

"I am going to use our bond to block out everything around you. It will be like a bubble, with only the two of us in it. You will be able to hear Xavier speak, but not via the bond, okay? Do not panic, it will only be temporary. I will give you an image, and when we get to the room with the coffin, I want you to open a portal to that place once we are ready."

We hadn't even gotten back into the castle, and the thought of removing the cursed box had already started me freaking out. Tugging his hand, I explained that we needed to stop so I could have the rest of the conversation without losing my marbles again.

We backed up a few steps until I had a clear head, and he finished detailing the plan.

"Better?" At my nod, he continued. "Xavier and I will perform an incantation to tie whatever magic that came with the casket to remain with it. Once we are finished and the portal has opened, we will send the casket through. You will close the portal while we clear the space of any residual spells. When we're done, we will return to the library and cleanse you as well."

"I don't understand. With the pendant, her magic is not supposed to affect me."

"Ah, but this is sneaky. This spell is not directly cast at you. There is a good chance that she crafted it to seek the scribe magic, or your mother's descendant. Because it is not being used to attack you directly there is nothing for the pendant to reflect."

"I wonder if it would be possible to put a drop of the potion onto the casket. Its intention is to null her magic..."

He looked thoughtful. "That may work. We will discuss the possibility with Xavier before we make any moves."

We stood silently for a moment under an old tree. For all the people and creatures on the castle grounds, it seemed remarkably quiet. My stomach did a tiny flip flop as his eyes met mine once more. While there had been absolutely no time for romantic interludes, it had become apparent to me that my feelings for him were growing stronger by the hour.

I actually looked forward to the time we would be able to stop worrying about war and destruction, and maybe even go on a date. I wanted to meet his family. Get to know him better. See where this whole "mate" situation would take us.

He grinned, and I blushed, realizing he could probably hear every last one of my thoughts. I attempted to hide by staring at the green grass below our feet, but he caught my chin and wouldn't let me.

The last thing I heard in my head was "Me too."

Then he kissed me, and all coherent thought went right out the window. Yep, we needed more time for moments like this.

All too soon, he stepped back and took my hand again. “Let's get to it, so we can make more of those memories together. The sooner we beat her, the sooner we can settle into a life together. I am putting up the block now, so don't panic if you can't feel the others.”

Xavier met us in the dining hall with food laid out.

“You are my absolute favorite brother.”

I sat and started stuffed my face without waiting for either of them and he laughed. “Well, seeing as I have absolutely zero competition, I would hope so.”

He agreed we should try the potion to see if it helped before we sent the coffin on its way. He didn't think it could hurt. At worst, it simply would have no effect on the spells, and we would continue with our original plan.

Meal consumed, we headed down the stairs. He unraveled the spells that had been laid on the door and we entered the room. It still lay there, looking innocuous as a stationary item could be. I uncorked the potion and dripped a single drop on top.

It had no drastic effect, but the air around it began to shift and shimmer. He instructed me to use another drop or two and when I did the spells broke. I actually felt them give way and disappear.

I knelt next to the coffin and cried. There, for all of us to see, lay my mother. Eyes closed, I couldn't tell if she lived or breathed, but she did indeed lie there.

Both of the guys gasped. “We need to call Celeste to consult quickly!”

I did and she said she would be with us momentarily.

“Hopefully we vanquished only the spells on the coffin, and not whatever spells may be cast over your mother. Luckily the potion did not actually touch her. We need to be sure we did not put her in any danger if she is in some sort of stasis.”

Celeste appeared by my side and gasped. “Amara.”

Chapter Twenty

At Celeste's instruction, I pulled my mother's tapestry into view. While intact, it appeared dull and without much color. Her runes sat empty and she had obviously been stripped of whatever she had not passed down to me.

Relaying what I saw, and didn't see, I did my best to give Celeste an accurate picture. After she had asked her questions, I opened my eyes and looked at her.

“Well? What should we do?”

“We cannot do anything until we discover the key to getting her out of the coffin itself."

Xavier looked pensive. "The potions nulled all her spells, correct? Perhaps she is held inside by magic only and we can just open the lid and transfer her to a bed?"

After a brief inspection, it became apparent that the creation didn't have a lid to open. It appeared to be crafted out of a single solid rock. Perhaps all we needed was a spell that commanded the crystal to release her. I voiced my thoughts.

"Before we do that," Celeste interjected, "we need to be sure you are prepared to heal her of whatever damage may have been done."

"I am not at all practiced on healing physical bodies." There was no way I would risk my mother's wellbeing on a skill I had yet to even attempt.

Xavier jumped to his feet from his position beside the casket. "Endryl! She is a healer."

"That's right..." I mulled it over. "As long as we are absolutely certain it is safe for her *and* the baby to enter."

He agreed. "I will also cover them both with a protection spell to ensure there is no doubt they will be safe. I'll find her and ask her if she will help us." He had made it through the doorway before he even finished the sentence.

I laughed. "He has it bad, I think."

Taryk grabbed my hand and looked at me with a twinkle in his eye. “It's not so bad, I think.”

Celeste hovered near us. “Everleigh. I want you to be prepared. It is possible that her body is no longer with us, and her soul is only tethered here via magic. If that is the case, there will be absolutely nothing we can do to bring her back to us.”

My shoulders tensed and my head began to ache at the very thought. But I knew she could be correct. “If that is the case, then I will be thankful we are able to free her soul and release her to be in peace.”

I choked slightly on the last few words, knowing my heart would break all over again if that were the case. But I also knew that I meant every word I had said. Whether she came back to us or went on to be at peace, she deserved more than being trapped in this horrid hunk of stone.

Taryk's thumb made slow circles against my skin as he held my hand, and I found it to be particularly soothing. I focused on taking deep breaths and centering myself for what may come in the next few moments. I could hear Xavier and Endryl approaching, and knew it would only be moments before we knew what the situation would call for. Healing or goodbyes?

Endryl walked right up to me and laid her hand on my shoulder. “I will do everything in my power to heal her, if she is able to be healed.”

My head bowed. “I know you will. And I appreciate that you are willing to help us.”

She gave my shoulder a tug, and I turned her way. “There is nothing I wouldn't do to help you if I could. You have given me everything. Returned my magic, my hope, and my child. I will be forever in your debt."

All I could do was shake my head, and I knew that she realized what I tried to convey. Turning to the others, I made sure we were all ready. They each took a place around the casket. We had agreed that Taryk would open it, so Xavier and I could be prepared for any magical intervention. I took one last deep breath and gave the go-ahead.

Taryk placed both hands on the top, murmuring quietly. For a brief moment, I panicked, thinking the box would not release her as we had hoped. Seconds later, the entire chunk of crystal had vanished, and she lay on the stone floor.

There was no movement or sign of life. Endryl immediately placed both hands on her, brow furrowed in concentration while I brought her soul into view. I pushed magic into her runes, hoping to somehow regenerate her being. I heard Xavier's voice as he, too, worked to bring her back to us.

It seemed that no matter how much magic I infused her with, there were no changes. At some point, I heard Endryl apologize. I felt one of them grab my hand, and I yanked it away. I would not give up yet. I wasn't ready. She just needed a little more time. More and more, I shoved the magic outward, willing her soul to wake up and the beautiful purple tones to return to it.

I didn't stop until I heard her say my name "Everleigh."

I looked up. She stood before us, not as a solid being, but an ethereal soul, just like Celeste.

"Oh, no, Mom. Please..." Rivers of tears fell from my eyes.

"Everleigh, listen to me. Your power has given me the strength to become visual, but I do not have long. Already the veil is calling me to the other side. I must go soon."

She closed the distance between us, placing her hands over mine. I gave her as much magic as I was able to prolong what little time we had left.

"I will pass to you all the knowledge I gained while in her possession. Use it to your advantage."

My eyes closed as I accepted what she offered. I did my best to compartmentalize and seal it away for now. I would examine her memories when I felt more stable. When she finished, I opened my eyes once more.

She now looked at Taryk. "Take care of her. The two of you together are unstoppable."

"You gave your life to save mine. I will never forget that, and I will honor your memory always. So long as I live and breathe, she will be safe." He too let the tears run freely.

"Xavier, my long-time friend. The dark mage will get what she has coming to her. I will always be grateful for your presence in my life. I'm so glad you and Everleigh have each other now."

Xavier's tears ran unchecked, and he could say no words. But my mother knew all he wanted to say.

She turned to Endryl. "Thank you for your efforts. Your child will grow healthy and strong. I have given my blessing."

She faced Celeste. “Thank you, for all you do for my daughter. When your time comes, I look forward to meeting with you again.”

Finally she looked at me once more. “I wish we didn't have to say goodbye. But this is the way things are meant to be. You have all of my love, and I will be with you always. You and Taryk make a wonderful pair. With your combined powers, you can be victorious. Have faith but be wary. Amass the largest army you can. She is strong, but you are stronger if you tap into your potential. I love you daughter. Thank you for setting me free...”

Her voice trailed off as she began to fade from sight. I tried pushing more magic into her runes but it was as if they had holes like a sieve; it just ran out.

“It is time, my child. She must move on.” Celeste's voice was gentle.

Wiping my tears, I stood. We would need to plan a memorial soon. For the moment, I just wanted to return to my room and be alone. I looked at the others. Before I could voice my thanks, I noticed Endryl looking pale and shaky.

“Endryl! We need to get you to bed. Xavier, help her!”

He picked her up in his arms and headed for the hall.

“Wait!” I stood beside him and opened a portal directly into her room. We needed to get her resting as soon as possible.

As soon as she lay comfortably in her bed, I perched on the edge next to her. “Let me give you more magic. Please. I can restore your waning energy."

She began to shake her head, but Xavier was quick to cut in. "Let her. If not for your sake, then for the baby."

She nodded, and her eyes fluttered closed. She had given much in her attempt to bring my mother back, and I would do everything in my power to be sure she was restored and comfortable.

Once she had been given a boost, she smiled at me. "I feel much better thank you. For now, I think I will take a nap."

Taryk and I left her to rest as Xavier fussed about her, offering to bring her food. It made me smile. I hoped things worked out between them. He deserved someone to make him happy.

As we returned to my room, Taryk insisted I get into bed and rest for a while as well. I would have argued, had I not been aware of how desperately I needed recharged. I needed to be at the top of my game from here on out. Sweats and sleep were the plan for now.

Soon, we would be gathering more volunteers and growing our army.

Soon, we would be moving forward with our plan of attack.

Soon, I would be meeting the dark mage face to face in battle.

But for now? I would take this moment knowing my loved ones were safe and protected, and I would close my eyes to rest. Tomorrow would be a new day.

The End.

Thank you for reading book two of the Soul Scribe Trilogy. Watch for the third and final book as we wrap up Everleigh's story to release near Thanksgiving.

I sincerely appreciate that you took your time to read my work! If you have enjoyed the book please consider leaving a review.

ABOUT THE AUTHOR

Tera Lyn Cortez has worn many different hats throughout her life: hospice CNA, booking assistant at the county jail, a district supervisor for UPS, plus Mom and Wife, to name a few. Being an author has always been on her bucket list!

She lives in the Pacific Northwest with her husband, five children, and multiple pets. When she's not writing, she's reading and spending time with her family!

Visit her website or Facebook page to make a connection!

http://www.teralyncortez.com/

http://www.facebook.com/teralyncortez

Made in the USA
Lexington, KY
11 November 2019

56846315R00151